"I doubt I'll get married."

"You have something against the state of holy matrimony?" Andy asked.

"Let's just say it's never been in my plans," Lori replied.

"Why wouldn't marriage be in your plans eventually? I can't believe you don't expect anyone to ask."

"Sure, I beat men off with a stick daily."

"Why does that not surprise me?" Andy said too seriously, despite his smile.

Lori sighed and reminded herself that her growing admiration for Andy had nothing to do with him personally. Falling for him would be a hopeless disaster....

D1413362

Val Daniels wrote her first romance in the sixth grade when her teacher told the class to transform a short story they'd read into a play. Val changed the bear attack story into a romance, and should have seen the writing on the wall. She didn't. An assortment of jobs, hobbies and businesses later, Val stumbled across a *Writer's Market* in the public library and finally knew what she wanted to be when she grew up. She suspects it will take eighty or ninety years to become bored with this career.

Val lives in Kansas with her husband, two children and a Murphy dog. She welcomes correspondence—with an SASE—from readers, at P.O. Box 113, Gardner KS 66030, U.S.A.

Santa's Special Delivery
Val Daniels

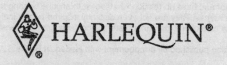

BABY BOOM

HARLEQUIN®

TORONTO • NEW YORK • LONDON
AMSTERDAM • PARIS • SYDNEY • HAMBURG
STOCKHOLM • ATHENS • TOKYO • MILAN • MADRID
PRAGUE • WARSAW • BUDAPEST • AUCKLAND

For Judy Christenberry, whose name should be the
definition of "friend" in the dictionary. Thanks for
everything, Judy—including the title.

ISBN 0-373-03534-9

SANTA'S SPECIAL DELIVERY

First North American Publication 1998.

Copyright © 1997 by Vivian A. Thompson.

Printed in U.S.A.

PROLOGUE

LORI Warren hummed along with the song playing on the bedroom radio. Her voice startled her as she actually sang a couple of the words aloud. *Joyful and triumphant*? Who, she wondered distastefully, had associated those particular words with the Silly Season? She frowned as she flipped off the radio.

She made her own concessions to Christmas, she admitted to herself, eyeing her reflection in the mirror and rubbing her lips together to blend the subtle glimmer of holiday gold into the rich burgundy color.

At least she looked good in one of the concessions: holiday colors. The bright, enameled holly earrings made her eyes sparkle even greener. The berries on the matching lapel pin were toned perfectly to the bright suit, and her short, stylishly cut brown hair picked up its reddish tint. She tipped her head this way and that to catch the light. She liked it. Maybe she ought to color it?

She gave herself an encouraging thumbs-up in the mirror. "And you're getting almost good at playing the game," she congratulated herself.

One last day. She could fake the cheer one last day, she comforted herself, then life would get back to normal. Well, almost normal, she modified. There were actually four more days until Christmas, but for the next three, she would hide. She wouldn't have to go to work and put on a happy face to fool anyone.

She'd hole up here, in her cozy apartment, and watch from a distance as all the world went crazy around her. Avoiding the mass chaos, she'd read the stack of books she'd been accumulating since before Thanksgiving—back when you could still buy a book that didn't feature some Christmas theme. Then people would become sane again.

Then in five days, she'd hop a plane to Denver and join the group of friends who had made a New Year's ski trip an annual tradition since their last year in college. Looking forward to that always got her through this manic season.

"Bah humbug!" she said with grim satisfaction, then grinned at her reflection.

If she didn't get a move on, she was going to be late. Her position in the city's convention and visitors' bureau was already on shaky ground. Her newly appointed boss was a bit intimidated by her knowledge and experience.

Turning off the lights, she grabbed her purse from the kitchen counter and her heavy coat from the small closet in the foyer of the apartment.

She stepped backward into the hall, automatically double-checking the door lock, and stumbled over something. She almost fell into whatever crowded her feet. Her hands flailed as she did a little dance in the two-inch heels and managed to regain her balance.

Great! She frowned at the knee-high cardboard box that had attacked her. One of her neighbors had evidently bought a nineteen-inch color television for Christmas…*and left the box for me to dispose of*!

She nudged it. The box seemed light, weighted on the bottom. They definitely hadn't left her the TV. Probably a pan of cinnamon rolls or some variety of homemade Christmas goodies, and whoever had left it had used all their reasonable-size boxes for wrapping presents, she thought sarcastically.

"I really don't have time for this," Lori muttered under her breath. Pulling back one top flap, she glimpsed a brightly colored patchwork fabric. Of course. Poor misguided Mrs. Jeffers down the hall had made her something.

Last fall, Mrs. Jeffers had invited Lori in to see the huge floor pillows she'd been making for all her nieces and nephews. She made all of her Christmas presents, the woman had explained proudly when Lori had oohed and aahed over the woman's skill. The compliments had probably earned Lori a patchwork floor pillow of her very own.

She'd check it out later, she decided. She and the boss were doing a presentation for a fairly important client at a breakfast meeting scheduled for nine o'clock. She couldn't afford to be late.

She groped in her purse for her keys and scooted the box into her apartment, far enough away from the door that she wouldn't stumble over it when she returned.

Something shifted inside. Moving the box had just rearranged the contents. No damage done. Lori shrugged and almost had the door closed behind her again when she heard a sound.

She widened the gap, flipped the foyer light switch and stared at the box in dismay. Kittens? Surely none of her neighbors would bring her kittens. Pets weren't allowed in this complex.

The weak, snuffley mewing came again. With a sinking feeling and an irritated curse for whoever had put her in this predicament, Lori approached the box again.

She couldn't keep it, but she ought to move the box into the kitchen and heat a saucer of milk for the poor thing before she abandoned it for the day.

Something jumped as she opened one flap and Lori started.

She shuddered, then peeled open another flap, tentatively this time. She could still only see the brightly colored fabric someone had draped inside. Well, at least whoever had packed this little surprise had been generous with cushioning. The quilt or whatever it was filled the bottom half of the huge box.

The mewing started again and grew louder. Unable to stand the suspense any longer, Lori jerked the last two flaps open. Whatever was inside sprang again.

Lori gasped in surprise, then fell to her knees.

The jumping thing was a tiny foot, kicking at a blanket. And the human baby, who'd only been tuning up so far, emitted an earsplitting angry cry.

"Oh, my God!" Tears gathered in her eyes. "Oh, God," she whispered again, "oh, my." She couldn't seem to quit repeating it. "Oh, my," she crooned, reaching automatically for the child.

Lori unstrapped the babe from the infant carrier that had been placed in the bottom of the box. As soon as she lifted and gathered the child to her shoulder, the crying started to ease. The sobs turned quiet, which was even more heartrending than the insistent crying. He snuggled and curled against her.

She wasn't sure how long she sat on the floor, the tiny baby against her chest. She only knew she was in shock. She knew the throwaway baby needed her warmth as much as she suddenly needed his.

A throwaway child.

A cap of dark hair curled slightly up at the ends and surrounded his face like a soft halo. His miniature head fitted into the palm of her hand. Tiny fingers curled and then spread spasmodically against her chest. He was so perfect, so…so helpless.

Lori couldn't stop shaking any more than she could stop the fierce, tender mix of emotions that spread from the tiny body straight into her quietly breaking heart.

The baby wiggled, turned his head, opening and closing his mouth. Even with her lack of experience, Lori realized the tiny thing was starving. She lowered him to her lap and settled him in the hollow she'd created when she'd dropped to sit, cross-legged, on the floor.

The baby flung his arms back, fighting against the imprisoning folds of the blanket, protesting his new position. His face contorted in fury. She wasn't prepared for the infuriated wail he let loose. The kid had lusty lungs. A positive thing, she decided. It must mean he was healthy.

"But I don't have a thing to feed you, sweetie," she said almost desperately. Surely, surely, she prayed, his mama wouldn't leave him without anything to eat.

Reaching for the top of the box, she tipped it over. Several things clacked together, then thudded against the cardboard side of the box and the well-cushioned floor.

With one hand bracing the screaming, squirming baby's tummy, Lori fished around a second blanket with the other. A handful of disposable diapers. She tossed them aside. A tiny outfit of some sort.

"How do women do this?" she muttered, feeling awkward and inadequate as she held on to him and worked one-handed.

The baby turned his piercing cry up a notch in volume as if berating her for wasting time with stupid, unimportant questions. He was hungry.

"I'm trying," she whispered, pushing the carrier aside and out of the way. The blanket came next, spilling additional diapers beside her. There, on its side, was a plastic bottle, filled and topped with a flat lid to keep it from spilling. "Thank you, God," she whispered.

She took the cap off and realized she had no idea what to do with it. Give it to the baby like this? Maybe she'd be able to think if he would stop screaming for a minute.

"It's okay, baby." She comforted him with a frantic pat against his tummy.

Two cans lay against each other in the bottom of the box. Applying a little more pressure to keep him where he was, she leaned on one hip to reach one of them. She read the side of the can, then cast it aside. No instructions? How could a can of formula not have instructions? It rolled back and clinked against the other one.

"Sorry, baby." He was strong, wriggling against her hand. But she was certain she detected his tiny body weakening. His cry seemed to hold less energy than it had only seconds ago. "This has to be okay."

She braced him with her forearm so she could use both hands to remove the snug cap. A minute later, she held the nipple to his mouth. He suckled once, then pushed at it with his tongue and turned his head.

She pulled it away. Oh, great! She *was* doing something wrong.

He opened and closed his mouth, still seeking. His chest rose and fell sharply a couple of times. His arms and legs stiffened and jerked. His face turned a rosy red. She knew she was in for another angry scream.

"Wanna try again?" she begged softly. "I don't know what else to do."

This time, he made a face, tried to draw away, then began a hesitant sucking. He accompanied the motion with the same quiet mewling that had alerted her to his presence in the first place.

What if she had just pushed the box inside, locked the door and went her merry way? She felt weak, thinking it might have happened that way. The knots in her muscles eased a bit as she sighed with relief. "It's a good thing you cried," she told the tiny, tiny infant, though she was no longer sure if she was talking to herself or the baby.

"Who," she exclaimed, "on God's green earth would leave you here? With me?"

The words reminded her of the slip of paper she'd seen beneath one of the milk cans. The baby continued to drink, oblivious to her movements now as she looked eagerly at the box again.

"There it is." The paper looked miles away and she noted her current limitations. How did you hold on to a baby, hold on to a bottle and do anything else? She lifted him carefully from her lap and into the crook of her arm. He was light, barely weighed anything. He couldn't be very old. Maybe a few days? Hours? she thought in wonder.

He watched her with unseeing, fuzzy blue eyes as she wiggled closer to the opening of the box. Hunched half in, half out of it, she wedged the bottom of his bottle between her neck and chin. Stretching as far as she could reach, she pushed at the cans and ran her hand along the bottom until her fingers felt a different texture.

"We got it," she said triumphantly, then dropped it to grab for the bottle that came loose when she spoke.

Adjusting him, the bottle and herself, she groped for the paper again. *We got it*! she thought. Her back felt as though she was developing curvature of the spine. Her arms ached. She scooted out of the box and wiggled back to lean against the door she didn't remember shutting. One-handed, she smoothed the folded notebook paper against her raised knee.

The message was in a carefully penciled print. *I know you won't let anything bad happen to my baby.*

The simple words swam before her eyes. She gulped at the lump blocking her throat. She blinked rapidly to push the tears away, then let them stream, unheeded, down her cheeks.

Kissing the tiny head cradled in her arm, she vowed, "I won't let anything bad happen to you." *I won't*, she promised.

CHAPTER ONE

ANDREW McAllister peeled the well-worn envelope from his door. *Hadn't his neighbors ever heard of Post-it notes*? With his thumb, he scrubbed at the small spot of residue left by the tape. As he inserted his key in the lock, he glanced at the original address on the recycled envelope. Lori Warren, Apartment 339, had been x'd out. His own name had been hurriedly scrawled above it.

Tugging at his tie, he slipped inside and set the note on the partition separating the foyer from the living room.

Lori Warren? This building, two floors up, he placed her address. He tried to remember meeting her and frowned when no particular face came to mind. Another neighbor attempting to bring him into their congenial little fold, he supposed. He'd deal with it later when he wasn't so rushed for time.

The wall clock on the opposite side of the room said he had an hour and twenty minutes to get to the most important Christmas party of the season—of his life. That wasn't much time when it was a forty-minute drive to the governor's palatial private home in the suburbs.

He made his way to the master suite.

Several people had assured him it was a huge coup to be invited to the private party the governor and his wife held in their home. But next year, Andy determined, he'd be going to the one in Topeka. The *official* one held at the governor's mansion.

He turned on the shower with one hand as he removed

12

his watch with the other. Allowing time for the temperature to adjust, he drew his tux from the back of the closet and removed the protective plastic bag the dry cleaners had covered it with. It looked okay, he assured himself. He'd had it cleaned last summer, the last time he'd worn it, but he'd been concerned all afternoon, worrying whether it might need a fresh pressing, cursing himself for not thinking to check it sooner.

He smiled to himself as he stepped under the hot spray sending huge clouds of steam out into the room and beyond. He knew as surely as he knew his name that worry over the suit was only a symptom. He wanted this appointment and knew he had only a slight chance of getting it.

He couldn't remember the last time his stomach had clenched and fluttered the way it had been doing all day. Maybe when he'd taken the bar?

His friends and fellow attorneys called him The Iron Man in court. He'd worked hard to establish the reputation. Nothing shook him. He didn't allow it. No one ever knew what he was thinking or planning.

Still smiling as he stood naked before the mirror to shave, Andy admitted that it had been a long time since he'd wanted anything as badly as the appointment the governor would be making early in the new year. Everyone, himself included, knew the invitation to this party was one of the governor's ways of checking him out.

You'll be fine, he assured himself, turning away from his image and quickly dressing.

When he returned to the living room, he was startled to find he still had fifteen minutes before he needed to leave. He dithered uncharacteristically next to the coat closet. He didn't want to be late but he didn't want to be the first one there, either.

The envelope that had been attached to his door

caught his eye. It gleamed in the soft recessed lighting. He picked it up, reaching to pull the note from inside. His fingers hovered at the frayed top edge as he realized the back of the envelope itself held the message in pencil, then pen. *Please! I don't know if I need a lawyer but I do know I...* The pencil lead had broken and blue ink took over....*need your advice*—advice underlined twice. *Please, could you come to my apartment? ASAP!* The ASAP was also underlined twice.

Lori Warren, it was signed. Apartment 339 had been added like an afterthought.

It's an emergency.

He almost missed the last. The small print crawled up the side of the envelope. At least there were no happy faces or Merry Christmases added in shaky, flowing script. Bertha Thomas, the elderly widow across the hall, liked to add those when she left him little informative instructions once or twice a week about the obligations and duties of apartment living.

He read the note again, adding a "desperately" where the pencil lead had broken. The word wasn't there in black and white, but he heard it in his head as clearly as if it were. The note screamed it.

Checking the time again, he grabbed his dress coat from the closet, flung it over his arm and patted his pants pocket to make sure he had his keys.

This—he fingered the envelope—would nicely fill the ten minutes remaining. He'd earn a few extra brownie points with his neighbors—not that he needed them. He wouldn't be living here that long—and this was probably someone panicky about too many speeding tickets. The advice he would give was quick and cheap: Slow down and pay!

Lori glared at the noisy thud at the door. It had been the worst—and best—day of her life and she'd just gotten the baby to sleep. She wanted nothing more than to crash in a chair and become a zombie for a few minutes.

Instead, she hurried to the door…and opened it just in time. His fist was raised to knock again. She didn't need this heavy-handed visitor hammering twice and waking the baby.

She didn't need *this* visitor at all, she thought as she felt her jaw drop. Tall, dark hair, dark eyes, with a sculpted face she was certain turned women to mush. Who *else* was going to turn up on her doorstep today? First a baby, now the gift from the gods she'd been fantasizing about.

She'd met him twice as she was coming out of the workout room in the basement of the apartment complex clubhouse. Sweaty and red-faced, both times she'd tried hard to blend with the woodwork and she'd prayed that she would meet him when she looked good. Why, oh, why couldn't she run into this man when she didn't look like something someone had pureed in the blender?

Third time's a charm, she thought caustically as her hand automatically went to her hair. She could feel tangles beneath the short sprigs that were sticking out in every direction. The red suit she'd never gotten around to changing felt sticky from nervous perspiration and baby formula. She had a run the size of New York City climbing the back of her hose.

And he was standing there in a tuxedo, looking so picture-perfect he could have stepped off the top of a wedding cake. She didn't know whether to drool or slam the door in his face.

"Lori Warren?" he asked, sounding as dismayed as she felt. Then he held up her envelope. "You left me this?"

"Mr. McAllister?"

He nodded, looking slightly startled as she grabbed his arm and yanked him into her apartment, closing the door behind him.

Her concerns about the way she looked were forgotten as tears formed in her eyes. "Oh, thank God, you're here. You will never guess what happened today and I don't...I can't—"

"Slow down." He held up an elegant hand. He used the same hand to touch the small of her back, half leading, half pushing her through the arch, past the low wall dividing the square foyer and into the small living room. "Come on. Let's sit down. You can calmly tell me all about whatever the problem is." He guided her toward the couch, stepping around the cluttered coffee table. He lowered his long length beside her as her knees gave out and she sat down.

She held her breath, studying her new neighbor. His hand on her back had felt reassuring. She felt adrift with it gone.

"Now," he said gently, "tell me what happened today."

She opened her mouth, then shook her head. She couldn't find the words. The tears that had flowed so freely all day started again. She tried to stop them but they kept right on rolling. They rattled her. She *never* cried.

Today, they'd spurted when the baby cried, spurted when she'd left the baby asleep and alone for two minutes to take the elevator down to place the note on his door, spurted every single time she'd thought about the baby—and she'd thought of nothing else—or read the note...

The note. That might explain what she couldn't. She grabbed it from the edge of the coffee table, gazing at it mindlessly for the hundredth time. She didn't need to read it. She'd memorized it. It didn't take much. Eleven words.

Eleven words that meant nothing, she realized, smoothing the note against her thigh. *I know you won't let anything bad happen to my baby.*

"I don't know what to do," she mouthed soundlessly, searching his face and eyes, hoping to find wisdom there.

Tiny lines formed between his brows as he stared at the paper she still held. "Maybe it would help if I read it?"

She hesitated, then handed it to him.

He looked up from the carefully lettered sheet of white stationery. The lines deepened as his scowl turned to a full-fledged frown. "You want me to keep something bad from happening to your baby?"

She nodded yes, then immediately changed it to a no. She felt her lips quiver and pressed her mouth with her fingertips.

"We *are* talking about a baby?" he queried. He glanced at the paper again. "Little thing about—" he held out his hands to the appropriate size "—so big?"

She nodded and gave him a tremulous smile.

"Then we're on the right track. I do know what they are," he assured her with a wink. His charming sense of humor made her feel almost sane.

The sanity went right out the window with the baby's cry from Lori's bedroom. She jumped up and ran from the room without another thought to her visitor.

On her knees in the middle of the bed, Lori checked the baby's diaper. She'd just changed it before she'd fed and managed to put the infant to sleep by sitting on the edge of the bed, swaying back and forth. That had been less than twenty minutes ago. Surely—

"What exactly are you expecting to happen to your

baby that a lawyer can fix?'' the man asked in a deep voice.

She glanced at the handsome figure who'd followed her and propped himself against the door frame.

"Have you been threatened? Is the baby's father trying to take him away from you?"

"It's a she," Lori corrected. She'd found she couldn't continue calling the baby a "him" when she'd changed her first diaper. She carefully lifted the babe and turned to sit down on the edge of the bed. Rocking automatically, she murmured softly and cradled the child against her. The baby immediately stopped crying.

If the past couple of hours had proved anything, they proved she *had* to trust someone. She'd thought she'd have an hour or two before the helpless being, who depended on her completely, woke again. Time to think. Time to figure out how to get more diapers. The baby was wearing the last one included in the surprise package this morning.

"It isn't my baby," she managed to whisper.

His back went ramrod straight. Those wonderful brown eyes sharpened. The light behind them said his mind worked quickly. They narrowed and directed suspicion at her. He was drawing the wrong conclusions!

"I didn't steal her," she protested.

His eyes widened. "You're keeping her for a friend?"

"Sort of," she prevaricated, unable to meet his gaze. "I found her. Outside my door. In that big box in the living room," she added.

"With the note." Understanding was beginning to dawn.

She rose, coming across the room carefully to protect the child from jolts. The tiny eyelids had fluttered closed again. The delicate mouth puckered and moved in the same motion the baby girl used to drink from her bottle.

Maybe the infant would sleep for a while if Lori just continued to hold her.

The visitor seemed stunned. Speechless.

Lori jerked her head toward the light streaming down the hall from the living room. "Come on. Let's go back out there. Will you give me some advice?"

He stepped aside, waiting for her to lead.

Lori eased down onto the edge of the couch. This time, he didn't sit down beside her. Mr. McAllister stood before her, hands stuffed in the pockets of his black trousers, ruining the elegant line of his impressive tuxedo.

He was the first one to speak. "When did you find her?"

"'Bout seven-thirty this morning."

"You haven't called the authorities?"

"I haven't told anyone. Except you now," she added. She wanted to be honest with him. Surely the what-you-get-out-is-only-as-good-as-what-you-put-in rule applied to lawyers as well as computers. Truth was the only way she could expect to get good advice, wasn't it?

"Why?"

"At first, I didn't have time. I was occupied trying to figure out how to take care of her." She realized she was still whispering. She cleared her throat. "Then I wasn't sure who to call, what authority. And, by the time I could, I wasn't sure if I wanted to call *anyone*. That's when I left the note for you."

His lips compressed in a solid, uncompromising line over those perfect white teeth. She glanced quickly away from him.

"Ms. Warren, you need to give me a retainer."

That brought her attention back.

"Are you hiring me?" he asked. His face looked carved out of stone. "If you are, you need to give me some money."

There was an urgency in his voice, something she couldn't ignore but didn't understand. Greed? Irritation set in so fast she had to consciously hold on to her temper and remind herself she didn't want to wake the baby. He didn't look nearly as good as he had a minute ago. She focused on keeping her voice calm. "Can you bill me? I just want a little bit of advice. I wanted—"

"Lady, if you're hiring me," he interrupted, "do it. Now."

So much for the rave reviews she'd heard from various elderly neighbors about the nice lawyer who'd moved into the complex. No advice without money, huh? She resented his obvious conclusion that she wanted *free* advice. Couldn't he bill her after the fact if there was a charge? One of the things she'd pondered at the back of her mind all day was whether she could *afford* a baby. She was living—barely—to the hilt of her income now. She would have to cut expenses somewhere, probably first by finding a less expensive apartment. She hadn't considered legal expenses.

She lifted her chin. "I don't know where I put my purse," she said, looking around. It wasn't on the kitchen counter where she usually set it. She'd been on her way out the door when she found the baby. She didn't think she'd touched it since then.

"This it?" He spotted it on the floor beside the arch leading to the foyer just as her gaze landed there. He lifted it and handed it across to her.

"Thanks." She juggled to open the wallet with one hand, then finally placed the open purse on the coffee table in front of her.

"Here, let me take the kid," he offered. In a second, before Lori could think about it, the child was in his arms. He plopped the infant against his shoulder, bracing her nonchalantly with one arm. Lori resented his casual confidence with the baby as much as she resented his greed. Life really wasn't fair.

"How much?" she asked stiffly, withdrawing two twenties from her wallet.

"Write me a check," he replied absently. "That would be better."

"Very well." She got out her checkbook and pen. "How much? Will a hundred do? You can always bill me if it's more," she felt compelled to add.

"Fifty should do it," he said. He patted the child as though he was an old hand at knowing what a baby needed. She looked smaller than ever compared to his hand. He glanced at his watch and grimaced as she handed him the check. He stuffed it in his pants pocket without looking at it. "Thanks."

She would swear the sigh he emitted was one of relief. She held out her arms for the child.

"Let me take care of her for a few minutes," he offered again, adding gently, "You look exhausted. Sit down. Take your time. I'll hold the young'un while you concentrate on telling me what you want me to do."

"Isn't that what I just hired you for? To tell *me* what I should do?" She couldn't keep the indignation out of her voice.

"No, ma'am." His soft chuckle surprised, then warmed her. "You hired me to keep us out of trouble."

So many questions popped into her head she couldn't begin to vocalize even one of them. Damn, he looked good, gazing at her with that devilish, killer smile—a direct contrast to the picture he made with the tiny baby against his broad chest.

"I have a feeling I'm about to see a crime committed," he continued.

Her frown grew.

"If you're going to admit to committing one, don't

you want our relationship covered by attorney/client privilege?''

"What crime?"

"To tell you the truth, I'm not sure," he said. "Kidnapping's the closest thing I can think of."

"I didn't kidnap her. She was left on my doorstep."

"Like I said, I don't know specifically what law you're breaking, but I'm confident that it's illegal to find someone's baby and just keep it. Am I right in guessing that's your plan?"

"That's what I want you to do. Tell me *how* to keep her. Legally," she added.

"You found her this morning?" he asked, scowling as he ran a hand through his thick dark hair.

"Yes."

"And you know you want to keep her? Some stranger's baby? A baby you can't be sure doesn't have something wrong with her? Do you want her if she's a crack baby or has AIDS or something?"

She looked at the child and silently prayed that she was healthy and normal. But even if she wasn't perfect, it didn't make a difference. It was something Lori hadn't thought of, but she'd take care of the tiny child, she thought fiercely. "Yes," she said again.

"What if the mother should change her—"

"It doesn't matter," she said, impatiently interrupting him. Maybe if the lawyer would quit looking at her with that subtle glimmer in his gaze, she could concentrate. "I want to keep her."

"Then, first things first." He moved easily to the end table, his movements not hampered at all by the baby. "We'll call the police, make a report and then we'll start the process of getting you appointed as her foster parent or guardian."

She moved faster than she had all day. "No." Her

fingers closed over his as he started to lift the phone. His startled look had her withdrawing her hand quickly.

The tiny child stirred against his chest and began the thing with her mouth again. The motion tugged at Lori, sucking out and exposing a vein of protectiveness she didn't know lay under the thick skin she'd worked so hard to develop. Lori resisted the urge to touch the baby. She probably couldn't do it without touching him again.

"As an officer of the court, I'm obligated to report criminal acts," he said softly. "If you hadn't retained me as your lawyer, I'd be reporting this abandoned child right now. And as your attorney that's what I advise."

An officer of the court. The very words set her on edge, stiffened her spine and made her move away from him. Money had never been as well spent as the check she'd just written. It bound him and defined him as *her* advocate. He couldn't do anything contrary to her wishes.

"Do this right, Lori Warren," he urged. "Report her to the authorities, then neither of us has to worry. I'll do my utmost to guarantee you're appointed her guardian."

"That's the problem. You can't guarantee anything." His brown eyes held steady on her, making her want to smooth her hair, rearrange her clothing. "Can you?" she tacked on the challenge.

"I'm very good at what I do."

"Then I'm glad I hired you." She had to be the one to break their visual connection. She focused on the baby. "But do you know where this baby would be right now if I'd called the police this morning?"

He frowned. "In foster care?"

She nodded. "By now maybe, but in the meantime, she would have spent the day being passed around frantic offices at the police station or social service agencies."

"By now, she'd be in a home," he said.

"With four or five other foster children and maybe an additional child or two of the family's," she said dryly. "Those are the kinds of places willing to take children in an emergency and at a moment's notice like this." She glanced at her watch. "And right about now, if the foster mother is any good, all of those children will be clamoring for her attention while the poor frazzled woman is trying to fix dinner."

"And if she's not a good foster parent?"

"The children are trying to stay out of the way and beneath anyone's notice." Lori made the mistake of looking at him again.

His brows lowered, matching the mouth that slanted in a concerned frown. "You're speaking from experience? You've lived in foster homes?" They were questions but his voice said he knew the answer. His eyes darkened with sympathy.

She raised her chin a smidge. "I survived. The system made me strong." She crossed the couple of feet that separated them and held out her empty arms. "That doesn't mean it has to be that way for this little one. Not if I can help it," she added determinedly as he handed the sleeping child over.

She tried to imitate the manner in which he'd cradled the helpless little girl—one-armed, between his neck and chest. She found herself leaning so far backward to compensate, she was afraid she'd pitch over. She gave up the attempt.

"Are you going to just keep calling her Baby or Little One?" he asked with an amused smile that turned into a thoughtful frown. "I'm surprised her mother didn't give her a name in the note."

Lori had been so busy trying to take care of the child, she hadn't thought about it. Of course, the baby needed a name. She felt inadequate all over again. "Any suggestions?"

He lifted a shoulder. "The logical choice would be Jane," he said. "That's what the authorities would be calling her. As in Jane Doe? That's what they call every female they don't have a name for," he added.

Jane Doe was as generic as Baby and reminded Lori of dead bodies in a TV movie. The thought validated Lori's decision not to report her to anyone. It hadn't occurred to her that they would call someone alive that. She shuddered. "I'm not calling her Baby Jane Doe."

"Maybe Rose?" he suggested. "You know, like a Christmas rose. You found her blooming at your door?"

Lori peered at the child. Her nosed crinkled in the habitual response she'd been trying to break ever since one of her foster mothers had pointed out that the frown would eventually cause wrinkles. She commanded her face to relax. "She doesn't look like a Rose to me."

"I think it's too early to tell," Andy said.

She glanced at him to catch the smile in his voice. "A name does seem like such an important thing. I should have thought of it."

He met her eyes in that direct way he had and his grin faded. "Whatever name you choose, it probably won't stick," he warned. He'd moved and was standing much too close. "In all likelihood—" he cleared his throat "—you are going to lose this child eventually, Lori. At least for a while. Are you certain you don't want to call the police now? Before you get too attached?"

"It's too late." His logic grated at her practical side, the side she tried to use when dealing with life in general. Unfortunately, even that commonsense side of her had deserted her today. She felt much too sensitive, too tender. She felt herself going on the defensive. "I can handle it,'' she said. ''Besides, you are going to help me. You're very good at what you do. Remember?''

''I remember.'' He touched her cheek, then stiffened and dropped his hand to his side. ''But I'd be a lousy lawyer if I didn't advise you of the probabilities.''

''I know. And I do appreciate it.'' The baby was an excellent excuse to move away from him, around him. ''I think she's wet,'' she commented.

''Can I get you a diaper?'' he offered.

''Oh, no.'' She closed her eyes. ''This is the last one. I forgot. I have to…I need…'' She let her shoulders droop and started over. ''Since you came here in that monkey suit, I know you didn't come here to spend the evening but…''

He winced as if the reminder was painful and checked his watch. She suspected whatever function he was supposed to attend was important. ''I thought this would be something minor,'' he explained. ''Something that would take ten minutes, but you just hired me as your attorney and I—''

''It's obvious you have other plans,'' she interrupted. ''I'm grateful that you came at all. You must be anxious to get…wherever. But could you stay, maybe spare ten minutes more?'' she pleaded, feeling guilty even as she asked. ''With the baby? So I can run to the store and get more stuff to feed her and some diapers? I'll hurry. I promise. I don't know what else to do. It's cold out and…and—''

''Let me go to the store for you.'' He held up a hand. ''It'll be quicker.'' He checked his watch again. ''Believe me,'' he added with a whimsical lift of his eyebrows, ''this has been much more interesting than the cocktail hour I'm missing. I'll get your things and still manage to make my appearance at the dinner. That's the important thing.''

She nodded and reached for her purse.

"The diapers and formula are my treat." He grabbed his coat from the end of the couch where he must have put it when he followed her to the bedroom. "What kind of formula did her mother leave?"

Lori hurried to get an empty can from the kitchen garbage. "Mr. McAllister..." she started as she handed it to him.

"Call me Andy." His dark eyes sparkled. "Might be better under the circumstance, don't you think?"

All day, she'd pictured the "Mr. McAllister" that people around the complex had talked about as a stern, older, fatherly, serious lawyer type. That image definitely did not fit this man. She felt her face grow hot, remembering her daydreams outside the apartment complex's exercise room. She prayed he couldn't read her thoughts now.

"I appreciate..." She shook her head, knowing she had to concentrate on what she was saying if she wanted to express her feelings adequately. She failed. "I do appreciate everything you're doing for us, Andy."

"How could I resist?" he asked softly. His gaze felt as physical as the hand he had rested on the baby's back. His subtle cologne wafted over to Lori. "I won't have but a minute when I bring back the diapers but I'll come back later, after the dinner, if you'd like. Will you and the baby be all right until then?"

She nodded with more certainty than she'd felt all day.

His thumb teased the corner of her mouth. "Smile. We *will* get through this." He winked, then raised his hand in a salute.

Lori watched the door close behind him. Speechless, confused by the crazy, erratic variety of emotions that had washed, one after another, over her all day, she stood rooted to the spot and experienced a whole new set of emotions.

She'd spent all her life trying to gain independence and become self-reliant. She'd finally achieved what she'd been striving for: she could say with confidence that she needed no one.

One tiny baby left at her door—someone who needed *her*—and suddenly, she was back where she'd started from. She needed and had to depend on someone else. She should find the thought abhorrent. She didn't. She was eager to accept help, she excused her optimistic feelings toward the man offering it, because of the baby.

She stroked the tiny head so near her own. She placed a soft kiss where her fingers had just been. "We'll take all the help we can get, won't we?" she whispered.

The baby wiggled her nose and snuggled closer.

"Now," Lori said, going back to the couch to sit down, "all we have to do is figure out how to take care of you. I have a feeling Mr. Flop-You-Around-Like-He-Knows-What-He's-Doing McAllister will be helpful there, too."

Even though they hadn't resolved a thing, the crushing burden she'd carried around all day felt lighter. And she hadn't cried like an idiot for at least half an hour. Lori sighed and relaxed.

He'd promised to come back later.

CHAPTER TWO

ANDY drove away from the governor's house, torn between despair that he'd done serious damage to his chances for the appointment by not making it to the cocktail party and anxiety to get back to the woman and the baby. Lori Warren was obviously clueless about taking care of a baby.

Which is why you should call the authorities.

He ignored the voice. Lori had taken care of the baby all day without anything disastrous happening. They'd be all right until he checked in on them again.

The voice refused to be silenced. *That's hormones talking if I've ever heard them*, it mocked him. *You liked the look of her, so you're justifying taking a retainer from her instead of convincing her to call the police.*

Andy smiled to himself. Okay. That *would* have been the logical thing.

But he'd seen those big red-rimmed green eyes and felt the urge to play Superman to her damsel-in-distress. He'd watched the distressed ditz who'd opened the door to him turn into a totally absorbed, frantically protective tigress, just because a baby cried.

He could still picture her kneeling in the middle of her bed, concern marring her perfect face. She'd unwrapped the child, examining her carefully from head to toe before cautiously picking her up and cradling her next to her breast. He'd rarely felt so moved...or as envious of some unknown man he'd believed to be the missing piece of a threesome. He was certain he'd never seen such undisguised love as he watched from Lori's

29

bedroom door. And as soon as he'd learned the facts, he'd felt as fiercely protective of Lori as she'd acted toward the tiny baby who wasn't even hers.

He shook his head as he turned into the entrance of the apartment complex.

White fairy lights decorated every tree and bush across the well-manicured grounds, looking elaborately festive but lacking in any direct hint of Christmas. His shoes echoed hollowly on the concrete as he made his way toward his building.

Disastrous, Andy defined the evening. Totally disastrous. From the minute he'd been admitted by the governor himself and escorted to the room where the rest of the guests were sitting down to dinner, to the moment he'd left, he'd endured the longest evening of his life. He should have stayed with Lori.

Andy tried to ignore the sinking feeling that by missing the cocktail party—and the little chat the governor had hinted he'd hoped to have during it—he'd eliminated himself from contention for the judicial appointment.

It didn't matter, he thought as he shrugged out of his tuxedo jacket. He wasn't a serious contender anyway, Andy'd been warned. The governor had a strong traditional streak. He liked to appoint older, bedrock-of-the-community-type judges who were solid family men. He had no way of knowing Andy had the strong traditional leanings but none of the trappings.

One thought renewed his optimism as he loosened his tie and threw his "monkey suit" on the bed. The governor wasn't expected to make a decision until late January, so Andy might have another chance to make a better impression.

Andy still had a chance.

*   *   *

It was almost midnight when Andy showed up at her door again. He knocked softly.

This time, the baby wasn't asleep and didn't look like she had any intention of going soon.

Lori's newly hired attorney looked weary, she decided, inviting him in. Tiny stress lines decorated the corners of his eyes. She hadn't noticed those before.

He'd changed his clothes. How could a man look as good in worn, comfortable-looking jeans as he did in a tux? she wondered. Revealing muscular forearms, he pushed the sleeves of his loose sweater up to his elbows as he sauntered past her into the small living room. "It's awfully warm in here," he commented.

"I don't want the baby to get cold." She gestured toward the baby seat she'd wedged into one end of the couch. "She's awake," she added unnecessarily.

The baby lay there, mostly staring off into space but occasionally kicking or flopping her arms up and down.

"Babies are comfortable if you are," he said.

"Oh? How do you know?"

He shrugged, frowning slightly. "Common knowledge, I guess. I don't know where I heard it," he added. "I just know it's true."

"I'll turn down the heat," she offered thankfully. She'd seriously been considering putting on shorts and a tank top if she ever got around to changing out of her cranberry-colored suit. As it was, she'd taken off the jacket and the hose as a concession to the heat.

When she returned to the living room, he'd settled beside the tiny girl and was softly talking to her. "Do you have your days and nights turned around, Baby?"

The tiny head turned toward Andy's low voice and she seemed fascinated. That makes two of us, Lori thought.

As if aware of her watching him from the doorway,

32   SANTA'S SPECIAL DELIVERY

Andy looked up and smiled. Amazingly, he didn't seem the least bit self-conscious to be caught talking baby talk—another reason to like him. "I don't suppose you've had a chance to figure out what you want me to do?"

"I've been thinking about it," she said. "Like I said, I want to keep her."

"For always?"

"For as long as she needs me to protect her." Lori faced him less warily. "I think that's for always, don't you? I'd like to adopt her."

He frowned. "That might be difficult since you don't have a birth certificate or any kind of parental release."

She came around the end of the coffee table and gazed at the little sweetheart. "And the state or social services do?" she asked, a touch of sarcasm slipping in.

"They have a way to get them." His patience didn't seem to run out.

"Yeah, they just declare whatever they want to be so. That's what I want you to do for me. Make them declare it 'so' for me."

"I wish it were that easy." He moved the baby seat from the end of the couch to the middle so she could sit down.

"Then that's what we have to do," she said, sagging onto the space he'd made for her. "We'll find her mother. We'll get a parental release."

The slow smile he gave her made her heart pick up a beat. "You make it sound easy."

"I..." She lifted one shoulder. Her throat tightened and her pulse continued to race erratically. "I *know* who the mother is," she defended her idea.

"You do?" He scooted toward the edge of his seat and leaned toward her, resting his elbows on his knees.

"I have to," she said. "Look at the note." She

glanced at the coffee table and the cryptic message lying there. "It starts, 'I *know* you...'" She paused for effect. "Whoever she is, don't you think she *knows* me?"

He sank back in his seat. "It says 'I know *you*, meaning *you*, anyone in the general public." His arm swept out in a broad gesture. "She was begging *whoever* found the baby not to let anything bad happen to her."

"It was intended for *me*. If it wasn't me, if she was just leaving her baby at any door, why didn't she leave her at yours? You're two flights easier to get to with a big box than I am."

"Good point," he conceded, his eyebrows rising as he straightened. "But that may have also been to get the baby away from the front door of the building. Her mother may have been protecting her from blasts of cold."

Lori felt her conviction waver. She had a feeling he was a very good lawyer.

"That also means she was in the building for a little while. Someone may have seen her. We can—"

"No."

He looked startled by her interruption.

"If we start asking questions, someone will report us," she said quietly. "Believe me, I thought about it. I thought about going around and talking to the neighbors this morning. But then someone would tell and we'd have to leave."

Andy scowled at her until she grew uncomfortable. "You've thought about who her mother might be?"

What started as a nod turned into a no. "It's another reason I can't tell anyone," she explained. "Her mother, whoever she is—" Lori smoothed a silky curl of the child's dark hair "—is in serious trouble now. Won't she be a criminal for deserting her child? Couldn't she go to jail?"

"She could," he agreed. "It depends somewhat on the circumstances."

"I don't want her mother in trouble."

"The court will take her situation and motivation into consideration. She may be very young," he offered as an example. "Technically, she didn't endanger the child." He grinned.

Good grief, he could make her heart stop with that smile.

"She left her in good hands," he continued.

"Oh, I wish I thought so," Lori wailed. "Oh, please, you have to help me with that, too," she begged. "I feel so lost. I have no idea how to take care of her. You seem to know about babies," she added hopefully. "Will you tell me everything you know?"

Visibly taken aback by her outburst, the man beside her quickly regained his equilibrium. "You haven't been around babies before?"

"You can't tell?" Her dry tone brought back his killer smile.

"There weren't any babies in the foster homes you lived in?"

"Well…" She grimaced. "There was a tiny one like this once, in one home," she said, "but we weren't allowed to touch him. Only the real kids could touch him."

"The 'real' kids?"

She felt impatient with him, reluctant to talk about this. "You know. The kids who belonged there. The family's *real* kids."

"You were never asked to help take care of him?"

"Not that one. Sometimes, in homes where there were older babies—you know, walking and starting to talk—we had to help. But, that I can remember, I've never been around or even held a tiny one like this. Oh,

and—'' the whole conversation suddenly reminded her
''—this baby still has that thing on her belly button.''

''The umbilical cord?'' he asked.

She nodded. ''Should I be doing something special
about that?''

''I'll show you later,'' he offered.

''Does it hurt her?''

''No.'' He reached toward her, then hesitated and
dropped his hand to the yawning baby instead. ''But it
tells us she's only days old,'' he said with the same awe
she felt in his voice.

The rush of warmth Lori felt toward him was scary.
She looked at him and hoped he couldn't see the stars
she was certain were in her eyes. She couldn't seem to
help it. Mr. Andrew McAllister was such a perfect mixture of practical knowledge, awe and concern, he intrigued her almost as much as the baby did. If she wasn't
careful, she could have a bad case of drop-to-her-knees
hero worship on her hands.

''How do you know so much?'' she asked as a caution
bell went off in her mind. ''Do you have children?''

His finger lingered on the baby's tiny hand. She batted
at it, then curled her miniature fingers around his until
he tugged. Her little hands flailed. ''I'm the oldest of
three kids, and my mom and dad were both from large
families.'' He made gripping and tugging his finger a
game with the baby. ''I can't remember a time when
there weren't babies around. Either new cousins, or now-
adays, nieces and nephews. Someone always has a baby,
it seems.''

''But not you?''

He grinned. ''Not yet, though I plan to have my share
eventually.''

She looked away, sorry she'd asked. She didn't want
to think of him with a wife and kids. Conversely, she

realized it would be safer dealing with him if he *was* married with a baby or two of his own.

"I've decided to name her Kris," she said quickly. Her voice sounded breathless. "You know, for Santa's other name, Kris Kringle. This is the best Christmas present he ever left me."

Andy opened his mouth, then closed it.

His troubled gaze made her anxious again. "You don't like it? It can be Kristine or Kristina."

"I think Kris suits her perfectly," he said so softly she almost didn't hear. "It's getting very late." He stood abruptly. "You and the baby should both get some rest."

"I know." She felt drained. Reaction, she knew, from the roller coaster of emotions she'd been on all day. "But we need to—"

"Tomorrow," he interrupted. "We can't do anything tonight anyway. I just wanted to check in and see that you were okay."

She touched Kris's face gently, then rose to stand beside him. "I forgot to ask. How did your thing go?"

"Okay, I guess." He made a face. "Do you need anything before I go?"

She shook her head. "I definitely have to go shopping for her tomorrow, though," Lori said. "I don't think I can keep washing one outfit out while she wears the other." She wrinkled her nose again. "But we're okay for the night, I think. We seem to be getting into a little routine."

He nodded wordlessly.

"Do you have any idea where I should put her to sleep? This afternoon, I put her on my bed, but—"

"You need a bed yourself. Make her one on the floor," he suggested. "A couple of blankets under her, one over. She'll be fine."

"Thanks."

He jammed his fingers in the back pockets of his jeans, looking hesitant to leave after all. The way he looked at her made her want to squirm or fill the silence with babble. Or both.

With a lengthy, clearly audible sigh, he swiveled and strode quickly to the door. "I'll be back first thing in the morning," he promised.

She hurried after him, nodding to his back. Her nerves were jumping crazily again. "You don't work tomorrow?"

"My calendar's clear until after the New Year." He faced her. "We'll have plenty of time to work on this little problem...and to teach you anything you need to know," he added reassuringly. His hand hovered near her face, then dropped to his side. "Get some sleep, Lori. See you both in the morning. Night, Kris," he called, winking at Lori as he firmly closed the door between them.

Lost in a reverie and a mishmash of emotions, she fingered the dead bolt instead of slipping it into place. She started when a soft tap sounded. He'd forgotten something. She smiled.

"You didn't look to see who it was," he lectured as she widened the gap between the door and its frame.

"Who else is going to be wandering around outside my apartment at this time of night?"

"Someone leaving babies."

His quip widened her smile.

"Here." He handed her a card. "You might need my number. I wrote my home phone on the back," he added as she studied the front. "But if you need me, they'll page me any time you use the front number."

"Thanks."

"And Lori..."

She looked up at him. The dark eyes mesmerized and confused her all over again.

"Don't hesitate to use it. Okay? Day or night. For anything."

"Okay."

This time he closed the door softly. She didn't move until she heard his footsteps go down the hall several long minutes later.

Nightmares! The woman, the situation, the whole damn day yesterday had given him nightmares.

And somewhere in there was the governor's dinner!

Andy dragged a hand across his face, trying to wake himself up. The phone rang and the sluggishness vanished.

"McAllister," he answered gruffly.

"Andrew?"

"Mom." As pleased as he was to hear from her, he felt a letdown. He should be relieved it wasn't Lori Warren. She wouldn't call unless there was a crisis. But leftover wisps of the nightmare made him antsy and uneasy.

"Did I wake you?"

"No, Mom, I haven't made it out of bed yet, but I was awake."

"Sorry," she said but didn't fool him.

He couldn't help but smile. The clock said ten after eight. Veronica McAllister thought staying in bed past daybreak was a sinful waste of time. Right now, she was probably patting herself on the back for rescuing him from an extreme case of sloth.

"So? Are you going to tell me? I'm dying to know how the governor's dinner went last night."

"I'm trying hard not to think about it," he told her. Not whitewashing a thing, he gave her the dirty details, including his less than optimistic thoughts on his chances at getting the judicial appointment. "I think he planned to talk to me during the cocktail party," he finished. "I was consigned to the far end of a massive table and the other candidate in attendance got the governor's undivided attention during dinner." Her indignant sympathy eased his disappointment.

Since the third candidate was not in attendance, the governor either knew him well—another strike against Andy—or the other candidate would be scrutinized on some other occasion.

"Why did you miss the cocktail party?"

"Something came up with a new client," he told her.

"Maybe you'll get another chance to meet with the governor."

"Maybe," he agreed skeptically.

"Well, the office is officially closed until after Christmas. That should help."

He kept his doubts to himself this time.

"When will you be home? You are going to stay a few days?"

Andy sat up on the side of the bed and heavy-handed his face again. "Listen, Mom, I haven't really thought about it. I'm only—"

"I know you're only ten minutes away, but Allison will be here with her kids tomorrow. Now that she and Jeff have moved to Texas, we don't get to see them often enough. Is it wrong for me to want all my children and grandchildren under one roof for a couple of days?"

"Will you settle for twenty-four hours?" Andy asked. "I promise, I'll stay at least one night while Allison's family is here. When is Melanie bringing her family over?"

He heard his mother sigh. "Christmas Eve."

"Then plan on me then, too." He was finally awake

enough that his mind was working. "Is there something you wanted me to help you with, Mom?" He'd bet that was the reason she wanted him there earlier than everyone else.

"I could use help hanging the greenery," she admitted. "Since John's hip surgery, I don't really—"

"I'll come by this afternoon," he interrupted. Making the promise and doing the work would be easier than trying to convince her Christmas would come whether or not she hung holly and ivy over every inch of space in her high-ceilinged rooms. "I don't really want him on a ladder, either."

He heard her sigh. "That's a load off my mind, Andrew. Thank you."

"You're welcome, Mom."

"But why don't you just stay?" she couldn't resist hounding him.

"The friend…the new client I mentioned is going through a bit of a crisis. I need to be available."

"We do have a telephone."

"I know, Mom, but—"

"A friend or a client?" Veronica broke in, picking up on his slip of the tongue. "Which is it?"

He realized he'd been thinking of Lori Warren as more than a client since the minute she'd drawn him into her dilemma. How many people would be so willing to take someone else's problem and make it their own? Change their whole life to accommodate it? He admired Lori's determination. He admired the caring he suspected had taken her by surprise. The more he knew, the more he admired. "Both, I guess."

"Is this a case I know about?" She almost didn't wait for his no before she continued, "A female?"

His mother was far too quick at reading things that

weren't there into other things. "Yes, Mom, but she's a client."

"And a friend," she reminded him. "Exactly what kind of problem is she having?" She sounded wary on his behalf.

"She's a client, Mom. You know I—"

"Oh, I get so tired of all of you reverting to that client-privilege thing when you don't want to tell me something. Why do you think I continue to work at the office as a receptionist a couple of days a week? So you don't legally have that excuse," she answered her own question.

Andy chuckled. Over the years, Veronica McAllister had been the sounding board for the ever-growing number of attorneys in the family. By mixing her keen sense for putting things into proper perspective with the ability to be dumber than a rock when warranted, she'd proved herself a valuable, hidden asset to the firm.

"I definitely will tell you about it later," he promised, then added, "Shoot, before this is over, I suspect the whole world may know about this baby."

"She has a baby?"

"Sort of."

"Sort of?" Her voice rose. "Either you have a baby or you don't."

"Mom." He'd said too much. "I have to go. I'll talk to you later, okay? Mom?" he said again when there was silence on the other end of the line.

"It isn't yours, is it, Andrew?" she asked.

"I promise. I'll let you know when I decide to have kids, Mom," he said dryly, then gently turned the screw. "Besides, aren't you the one who keeps hounding me to have kids?"

"I want you get married first." She was carefully indignant.

"You don't always say that," he taunted her.

"Well, you don't have to worry about that again," she promised. "I will be very specific in the way I phrase my nagging from now on."

"Do that. I'll see you later, Mom," he said, then hung up quickly before she could think of another array of questions and demands.

His smile died as he looked at the clock again. It was past time he checked in on Lori Warren and baby Kris.

He must be as crazy as she was, he decided as he took a quick shower and dressed. The woman didn't have an inkling how to take care of a newborn. If something happened to that baby...

The horrid dreams that had plagued him on and off all night surfaced to haunt him again. He *knew* they were purely a product of his imagination. He *knew* her throwaway remark about the need to leave was just that—a throwaway remark—but that didn't help. When he was dressed, he didn't even take the time to make a cup of instant coffee. Surely Lori would have coffee made.

By the time he made it to her door, he'd managed to calm himself again...until he knocked and didn't get the slightest response.

He listened for a minute and didn't hear a sound inside. Maybe they were both still asleep. He hesitated knocking again.

No, newborns didn't sleep this long into the morning. His sisters' kids were always up at daybreak. His light tap received no response. He pounded harder. Still no answer.

Increasing the tempo and the intensity, this time he also called her name. "Lori."

"Is something the matter?"

Andy jumped a foot. He didn't recognize this neighbor. With her hair in rollers, he wasn't sure he would know the older woman even if they'd met before.

"Do you know Lori Warren?" He automatically pointed to her door.

"Sure." The woman looked ready to launch into a history lesson.

"Have you seen her this morning?" he asked hurriedly to forestall it.

"No, but I heard her coming and going in the wee hours of the morning. Woke me up."

An alarm went off inside him. "What time was that?"

"Around one o'clock."

He breathed easier. The woman had probably heard him leaving.

"Then again around three-thirty or four. I couldn't believe she was out and about so early. Nothing would have been open."

"But she's here now, don't you think?" He was frowning, knew he'd added the "don't you think" for his own benefit.

"Don't know." The woman widened the gap in her door. She wore incongruous fluffy cartoon characters on her feet. "I haven't seen or heard her this morning."

He felt her watching as he pounded the door again. Despite the chill in the semiheated hallway, he felt sweat bead on his brow.

"I'm sure she doesn't sleep *that* sound," the woman called over his knocking. "She might not be home. Maybe she went somewhere for Christmas."

"Thanks."

She nodded and quietly shut her door.

He leaned against Lori's. His nightmare had featured a woman with Lori's voice. He replayed it in his head. The woman called his name. He heard sirens. A baby's cry. But the woman always remained out of reach, out of sight, hidden. Swamped by the same sense of desperation that had jolted him awake several times during the night, he flattened his ear against the door and listened.

Nothing. Not a single sound from inside. He caught and discarded several ideas about where she could be.

The neighbor's door opened again. "Listen, I know she was meeting friends in Colorado *after* Christmas. Don't think I heard her say when she planned to leave. Maybe she went early," she offered helpfully, eyeing him with concern. "Are you okay?"

"Fine. I'm fine. Thanks for your help," he added again, already dismissing her from his mind.

"Anytime."

He stopped her again when she started to close the door. "You don't happen to know what kind of car she drives?"

The woman's scowl moved the rollers forward on her head as if they had a life of their own. "Some little red thing. I'm not sure what kind exactly but I'll get my husband if you want. He'd know."

"That's okay." He was going to have to convince the complex manager to let him in her apartment anyway. The kind of car Lori drove would be on the manager's records somewhere.

The neighbor stared at him another second, then seemed to decide he'd disrupted her day enough and closed the door.

Wearily, Andy eyed Lori's door again. He'd thought she trusted him. But he hadn't been very reassuring—obviously not enough anyway. But how could he reassure her? She knew from experience what little Kris could expect if she hit the "system". Lori's nightmares were probably more vivid because they were based on reality.

His nightmare had come true. Lori had taken the baby and run.

He pushed himself away from her door and mentally noted a course of action. With help from a few friends in appropriate places, maybe he could find her before any real damage was done, before she was in real trouble.

This offense, he was certain, had a name. If he had to call the authorities in, they would label it kidnapping. Poor Lori Warren would be in trouble as serious—or worse—than the baby's mother.

With all his heart, Andy wished he'd reminded Lori before he left last night that she couldn't help little Krissie from a jail cell.

CHAPTER THREE

"SHE'S probably Christmas shopping," the pretty young manager told him with a bright smile when they couldn't find Lori's aged red Ford Escort in the Building Three parking lot.

"I don't think so," Andy said. The pit of his stomach felt like he'd swallowed a rock. It flip-flopped heavily. "I don't think she's exactly one of Santa's little elves," he muttered under his breath. "She doesn't even have a Christmas tree."

"What?"

"Nothing. I'm talking to myself." Come to think of it, he hadn't seen a thing in her apartment that hinted she gave a nod to the holidays, not even a Christmas card. The only seasonal thing he'd noticed were those ridiculous holly earrings she'd been wearing. They'd caught his attention because they matched the green of her eyes.

"Just because her car isn't here, that doesn't mean something disastrous has happened," the manager said.

He repressed the retort he wanted to make, refusing to perpetuate the friendly argument they'd started in her office. "No, it doesn't." If Lori'd had an emergency and was able to get help, she would have called him.

She *would* have called him if the baby was sick or something. Lori was just too uncertain of her own judgment where the infant was concerned.

"I know there are a million places she could be," he said diplomatically. "I just don't think she's at any one of them. Something's wrong. We need to check her apartment.'' Maybe he could get some hint of where she would go.

The perky woman rested her gloved fist on one hip. ''There *are* laws.'' Her words formed a cloud around her face in the frigid morning air.

''I know. I'm a lawyer, remember? *Her* lawyer,'' he emphasized. ''You wouldn't want to find out a week from now that something has happened to one of your tenants? That you could have helped but didn't?''

She frowned, blinking uncertainly.

He took advantage of the interested gleam he'd seen in her eyes when he'd first walked into her office. It had dimmed when he started asking questions about one of her female tenants. He beamed his most dazzling smile at the young woman and struggled to remember the name on her office door. ''If Ms. Warren didn't have problems to begin with,'' he said, pausing to let the woman with him note how he formally distanced himself from Lori, ''I might not be so concerned, Monica. As it is…''

Her eyes narrowed. She reached in the pocket of her wool coat and brought out a ring of keys. ''Okay,'' she said. ''I'll let you in. But you have to promise to take the blame if she's upset.''

''No problem.'' He waited to exhale his relieved sigh until she started toward the apartment building.

''Listen…'' She turned to look back at him as she continued to walk. ''She isn't in the kind of trouble that will cause problems here, is she?''

''You mean police raids, sirens, that sort of thing?''

She flashed him a nodding smile. ''We do try to keep things civilized here.'' Her level gaze held his until she reached the curb and had to look down to step up onto the concrete sidewalk.

''Her problems are legal, not criminal,'' he assured

her. *Unless she's kidnapped the baby and run.* He didn't want to think about it. His involuntary shiver had nothing to do with the freezing morning air.

Apartment 339 was as unnervingly quiet as it had been before. The manager knocked several times while Andy crammed his fist in his pocket and waited beside her. The door behind them opened a crack and he could feel Mrs. Hair Rollers peering at them.

"Ms. Warren?" the manager called. She reverted to saying, "It's Ms. Wilson, the complex manager," after the first knock. Finally, she inserted her key.

Andy held his breath. His first glimpse inside told him it looked as though a tornado had struck—pretty much the same as it had looked when he'd left last night, except the tower of crumpled paper towels and napkins on the coffee table was smaller than it had been. She'd been using those as clothing protectors yesterday.

"Lori?" He hurried past his companion.

"What a mess," Ms. Wilson said, following him in.

There were dishes scattered about. A bottle here and there. Lori's red suit jacket filled the seat of the one easy chair in the living room. A pair of hose dangled from an end table. The box Kris had been abandoned in sat on its side in the doorway between the living area and the small dining area.

"She had a very bad day…" His defense of Lori was left unfinished. She was there, lying on the couch. Her short dark hair stuck up at odd angles on the top of her head. Her long dark lashes decorated the blue shadows beneath her closed eyes. Both emphasized a deathly pale face. "Lori?"

She didn't move. A blanket half covered her faded chenille robe and half hung over the side of the couch. Her arm was extended over the edge and her hand rested on little Kris, who lay on her own square of blankets on the floor.

"Lori," he said again, louder this time.

"Is she all right?" The manager's nervous voice startled him. He'd forgotten her. She'd stepped up close behind him.

Gas. What if there was a gas leak? His heart thudded heavily until he reminded himself that the complex advertised "total electric living".

He looked down at Kris. Her tiny chest rose and fell normally. She looked like a normal sleeping baby.

With a hand that felt cold as ice, he reached out and touched Lori's face. The silken skin beneath his fingertips was warm and reassuring. He released a big sigh of relief. A strange fury grew to take its place. As relieved as he was to find them both here, alive and well—they were both fine, he affirmed—he was mad as hell. At her. At himself.

What in heaven's name had he been thinking? How could he have let this woman, who slept like the dead, accept responsibility for a newborn baby? Who wouldn't wake up if the child was screaming her lungs out? And when Lori *did* wake up, would she have any concept of how to handle whatever problem there might be?

"Lori." His voice was as gruff as he felt. He nudged her shoulder, hesitant to do more than poke at her out of fear that he would grab the woman and shake her silly.

Lori sighed and turned away from him. The hair on this side of her head was flattened against her face.

"Lori," he said again with another poke. Andy crossed his arms and stood back to watch with an almost morbid curiosity. His grip on his biceps tightened.

Dammit! The woman *did* sleep like the dead.

"Maybe we should call 911."

"They're both fine," he muttered. "Like I said before, Ms. Warren had a very trying day yesterday. I'm sure she's just exhausted." He shouldn't have left her last night.

And Miss Perfectly Proper Manager was looking at him with a bewildered, uncertain gaze. "If you're sure they're okay, maybe we should just leave?" Her voice rose, turning it from a statement into a question midsentence.

"I'd better stay in case the baby wakes up," he said, clenching his teeth. "Someone has to take care of her."

"That's another th—"

The baby whimpered quietly, as if she'd heard Andy mention her and wanted to respond.

Before Andy could make a move toward her, Lori's eyes popped open. She kicked at her blanket, swinging her feet to the floor as soon as she was free. She didn't notice either of them until she bent to reach for Kris. He knew the second Lori spotted their legs because she froze.

Andy could see the jolt in her eyes as her brain kicked in, putting shock in her gaze as she looked up. Frowning concern replaced her surprise as she glanced from him to Ms. Wilson. "Is...is something wrong?" Lori managed to ask in a rusty morning voice.

Kris's whimper turned more insistent.

Lori finished the task of picking her up, showing more confidence in handling the babe than she had yesterday. She braced the child against her shoulder and wrapped the other arm around her protectively. The child quieted.

They must have spent a rough night, Andy thought semisympathetically.

"Is something wrong?" Lori asked again, this time turning her attention to the apartment manager as she patted Kris's back and swayed methodically.

"We couldn't wake you," Andy answered for them. "I thought something might have happened," he added, torn now between wanting to shake her and gathering them both in his arms in pure relief. "I got Ms. Wilson to let me in."

Something sparked in Lori's green gaze. Annoyed green daggers shot at him before she glanced quickly away. "Well, I thank you both for your concern." Her voice softened as Kris began to fuss again. "But we're fine. Or we will be as soon as I get her a bottle."

The apartment manager seemed to be coming out of her daze.

Lori rose, straightened her back and lifted her chin. "If you'll excuse me."

"I'm afraid I'm going to have to increase your rent, Ms. Warren," Monica Wilson said beside him.

Lori stopped in midstep. The dangerous glint in her eyes landed on him before she looked away in disgust again. The air around them was thick with an emotional charge.

"You know..." The apartment manager's voice had risen a notch. It sounded shrill. Andy cringed. "There's an additional charge for tenants not on the lease in this complex," she finished. "You signed—"

"I know who's in my lease," Lori said. "I plan on finding another place anyway. I assume you will give me time."

"She's just keeping the child for a few days," Andy protested, and both feminine stares swung back to him.

Fire! The daggers in Lori's eyes turned to angry green fire. Getting the manager had been a major offense but saying she'd only be keeping the child a few days had enraged her. The concerned interest in Ms. Wilson's gaze was much easier to take.

"She's taking care of little Kris for a friend," he ex-

plained in a calm, measured voice. He didn't dare look
back at Lori. He could still feel the pricks of her anger
and was afraid she would contradict him, get herself in
trouble—just what she didn't need right now.

Don't rock the boat, Lori, he begged with a silent
look, then glanced at the still-open door. The hair-
rollered matron had dressed and stood in the hall, watching with interest.

When he refocused on the two women in the apartment, little had changed, although Lori's chin may have
squared more stubbornly and risen another indignant
inch.

"Is that true?" Ms. Wilson asked. "You're keeping
the baby for a friend? She looks awfully...brand-new."

"Part of the problem." Andy drew the woman's attention to him. "The baby's birth was very difficult. Her
mother can't take care of her right now." Andy was
fairly certain he hadn't told a single untruth...yet.

The apartment manager sent a sympathetic frown in
the baby's direction. "Oh?"

"We're hoping she'll be much better soon." He decided he'd better get Monica Wilson and Mrs. Hair
Rollers out of the picture before Lori let go and said
something she shouldn't. She definitely didn't need an
audience if that happened.

He put his heart and soul behind the smile he gave
Ms. Wilson as he crossed the room. Grasping her arm
lightly, he pointed her toward the door.

Lori jiggled Kris, whose cry was gradually changing
to a healthy, hungry scream.

"Monica," he said, lowering his voice, "I don't know
what I would have done without you. Thank you for
your assistance." She was walking with him. "I'm sure
you understand my concern now."

Behind them, he heard Lori move toward the kitchen.

Ms. Wilson's frown deepened. "So is there a legal problem with the ba—"

"I owe you," he interrupted, saying the first thing that came to mind. "Dinner. Let me take you out to dinner at the very least."

The legal problems became a vague memory. Monica Wilson's eyes brightened with feminine interest again. "Just doing my job," she said coyly, but her head tilted as she waited for him to press. Her smile developed a dreamy quality he suspected she practiced before a mirror.

He had her outside the door. He saw a crack in the apartment door across the hall. A couple of inches below a bright purple roller, an eyeball watched them. "Everything's okay," he assured her. "Thanks for your help, too." Her door clicked shut immediately and he turned his attention back to Monica Wilson, who waited expectantly. "I'll come by the office after Christmas. We'll arrange something."

"I can't wait."

"Good. Thank you again. You've been a great help. Talk to you soon." With another forced smile, he quickly closed the door between them.

He was exhausted. He eyed his watch. It was barely after nine, he felt like he'd run a marathon...and he wasn't through yet.

Kris's cries had stopped. Lori must be taking care of the child's needs. He squared his shoulders and guessed he'd better find them.

How could facing one small woman with her arms full of baby sound as daunting as facing a lioness in the lion's own den?

The front door closed and Lori watched the opening between the kitchen and the living room with a growing sense of betrayal. She could hear him coming. Slowly. Treading lightly.

She glanced down at Kris. The baby looked past the bottle at her with blank and unassuming trust. She couldn't get too heated with him, Lori reminded herself. She had Kris to think of.

The footsteps stopped at the doorway and Lori looked up.

"Listen, Lori, I—"

"You can leave now," she said with as much cold disdain as she could muster. It wasn't easy. He looked like a guilty little boy with his dark hair falling over his brow and his brown eyes wide with contrition. "We're fine."

"I was worried. In my place, you would have—"

"With friends like you, I don't need enemies." She hunkered over the child, wishing she could curl around her, sheltering her from everything—including the lawyer Lori had hired to protect them. "I should be grateful you didn't call the police, I guess."

"I couldn't wake you. What was I supposed to do?"

She finally met his eyes again. "Let us sleep, maybe?" The saccharine-sweet sarcasm hit her target. How dare he flinch as if she'd wounded him? He was the one who had betrayed—

"And what if something *had* been wrong, Lori?" he interrupted her thoughts. "What if there was a gas leak or some—"

"Is that possible?" She glanced back down at the baby. "Every apartment in this complex has electric appliances and heat."

Suddenly, his shoes were in her line of vision. She didn't want to look up at him and was still debating it when he crouched in front of them.

"Lori, put yourself in my place." His brown eyes

were coaxing. "What kind of friend—or lawyer—would I be if I didn't care if something was wrong?"

She compressed her lips and stared at him.

"I knocked and banged and pounded on your door. No answer. I disturbed your neighbor." He waved a thumb in the direction of the front door. He scowled as if he suddenly remembered something. "What were you doing out and about at 3:30 this morning?"

Her frown answered his, then cleared. "Trash was taking over my apartment," she said stiffly. "Kris was finally asleep. I realized I might not get a better chance. I ran down to the Dumpster." Not that it's any of your business, she wanted to add.

"The neighbor heard you going in and out. I couldn't wake you this morning. And I was supposed to assume you were sleeping? That you both were fine?"

She felt herself weakening. She took refuge in sarcasm again. "Oh, so you went and got the manager, decided it was okay to get me in trouble there? What makes you think I can afford to pay higher rent *and* the additional expense of keeping Kris? I know I'll have to move anyway—get something bigger, less expensive—but I hoped I could hold off until things are more settled."

"I didn't think about your lease, Lori. I wasn't thinking about mundane things. I was thinking about you." He seemed so sincere. So concerned.

"So you totally ignored *my* concern about it and reported me yourself."

"I was thinking about the baby," he added quietly.

She resented him knowing her soft spot.

"What if Kris had needed something and you didn't hear her?"

How could he use Kris against her?

"I didn't convince Ms. Wilson to let me in until we couldn't find your car in the lot," he continued.

"My car wasn't in the lot?" Her fury with him was suddenly secondary. "My car wasn't in the lot?"

Cradling Kris against her breast, she rose and made her way across to the sliding glass door that opened onto a small balcony. Normally, she would have opened it and stepped outside. One quick glance at the baby changed her mind. Babies and freezing cold probably didn't mix.

She drew the vertical blinds and plastered her face against the glass. From the balcony, she had a clear view of the section of the parking lot where she always parked. From here, she could just see the corner. "It's there," she protested, looking at him, then leaning back to double-check. "It's there."

Kris watched her with a wide-eyed, what's-this-all-about? fascination. Andy had taken her place by the window.

"Where?"

"There. Second from the end of the front row."

He frowned. "The black Mustang?"

"That's my car," she assured him. "Or at least it will be when I make all the payments."

"Monica said you drove a red Escort."

Lori raised her eyebrows at the use of the apartment manager's first name. The stab of unpleasant emotion wasn't jealousy, she reminded herself. It was indignation. She'd named the feeling while he'd made his date with the airheaded apartment manager as she changed Kris's wet diaper. He was supposed to be on *her* side. She was incensed at his betrayal.

Andy stared at her strangely. She lifted her chin and picked up the thread of their conversation. "I didn't think to tell anyone in the office when I traded cars this fall," she defended. "That's surely not a crime."

Kris drew her attention with a noisy sucking sound. The formula was gone. Bubbles formed and expanded inside the bottle. Lori pulled it away and waited, watching to see if Kris was satisfied or if she was still hungry and would start crying again. After working her tiny mouth for several seconds, she started to squirm.

"She needs to be burped," Andy said.

Lori knew she scowled. As he stepped toward them, Lori remembered. She'd seen people do this before. Throw the kid up over your shoulder. Pat their back sort of hard.

Andy grabbed a dish towel from the drawer pull near the sink where Lori kept it hooked and spread it over her shoulder.

His touch was warm, caring. She didn't want to feel it. She concentrated on turning Kris up to her shoulder. "I haven't been doing this. What happens if you don't? I haven't done her permanent damage, have I?"

"No." Andy smiled. "I think their little tummies get upset. They get fussy."

That might explain why Kris had been cranky most of the night. Lori imitated her mental pictures and Andy nodded his approval. She turned her thoughts to her car once more. Something niggled at the back of her mind. "Why did you think it was a problem that my car was gone?"

"I thought there may have been an emergency. I thought you may have had to take the baby to the hospital or something."

He answered too quickly. He gazed at her too steadily, then looked away too pointedly.

"You think I wouldn't have called you if there'd been

an emergency? Isn't that why you gave me your phone number?"

"I wasn't certain you would."

"I would have *had* to call you—my legal adviser—wouldn't I? Taking her to the hospital would be like reporting her to the police. I wouldn't have a birth certificate or insurance or anything."

"I was worried," he added for the umpteenth time. He glanced away when their eyes connected.

"Don't you think I've considered those things?" She paused. "I've thought of little else. It scares me to death," she ended, almost beneath her breath.

Kris emitted a belch that was bigger than her whole little body. Even that crude sound filled Lori with a fierce protectiveness she couldn't begin to describe. The emotion frightened her as much—or more—than the responsibility she'd taken on.

"You surely understand why I was concerned when I couldn't rouse you," he said, reading her mind.

He was right. She understood. But she didn't have to admit it out loud. Something still bothered her and she frowned.

"Whatever else you think, I don't want anything bad to happen—" he borrowed the words from the note "—to Kris *or* you, Lori," he added. "That was my concern."

The missing piece of the puzzle slipped into place. She gazed at him in disbelief. "You thought I'd taken the baby. You thought I'd taken her and...and...run." She hadn't taken the time to hide her hurt. She cloaked it now.

"That's what you told me last night."

She scowled.

"You said someone would tell and you'd have to leave."

She snorted as she realized what he was talking about. "I said if someone reported us I'd have to leave. The apartment," she added derisively. "I can't afford the extra rent they charge for additional occupants. I can barely afford this place now. You think I'd kidnap her? Do something so irresponsible?"

"Think about it, Lori." The sparks in his eyes looked ominous. "What the hell do I know about you?"

She couldn't think of a thing to say but she managed to recover her cool gaze.

"I don't even know how old you are."

"Twenty-seven," she filled in.

"I don't know where you work or what you do. I don't know who your friends are—or even if you have any."

She didn't attempt to answer his questions. He didn't give her a chance.

"I don't know where you've been or where you're going." He took a deep breath. "For all I know, you could have been in jail ten times and secretly killed off two husbands."

"I *have* been busy, haven't I?"

He ignored her snide comment. "I don't know if you're romantically involved with anyone. If you are, where the hell is he? Where are your friends when you need them? Why did you turn to me?"

She wished with all her heart that she hadn't. She stared at him mutely but felt the pain grow and stab at her.

"It might be easier to tell you what I *do* know."

He paused but she refused to waste energy responding.

"I know you live in an apartment in this upscale, mostly adult complex but I don't know how long you've been here. *Now* I know you drive an almost-new black

Mustang and are making payments. I know you spent some time in foster homes while you were growing up. I don't know why or how many or how much time. It doesn't sound like it was pleasant.''

"It wasn't all bad," she found herself returning. "I had positive experiences, too."

"Good." His expression softened. "That about summarizes what I know—except that you found a newborn baby and are determined not to give her up. And I'm fairly certain you've never had a baby because you don't have the slightest idea how to care for one," he added wryly.

"I'm learning," she defended because she couldn't help it.

His shoulders slumped. His voice lowered. "I also know you and that kid gave me nightmares last night. I kept dreaming you ran away. You were always too far away, out of reach. When I woke up, I wasn't in the mood to find 'no one home'."

They stared at each other for what seemed like hours. Kris finally squirmed, breaking the silent spell that had fallen over the room.

"I trusted you," Lori said quietly.

She took her eyes off him for seconds, just long enough to wipe the drool from Kris's button-size mouth. Somehow, during that instant, he moved closer. Too close.

Then he touched her. He caught a tear she didn't know was there from the end of her eyelash. He ran the back of his finger down the side of her cheek and along her clenched jaw. "You don't trust easily, do you?"

"No." She moved away.

"I'm sorry I didn't trust you back," he said in a voice that made her want to cry.

"Why didn't you just turn me and Kris in?"

"Believe me, when I couldn't rouse you this morning, I was wondering that myself." His lips compressed in a thin, thoughtful line. "Especially since I've racked my brain and can't think of a single action we can take."

"What do you mean?"

"Essentially, every legal step I can think of will be the same as reporting her as an abandoned child."

"And that means?"

"The red flags go up. The state steps in and becomes her guardian and..."

"And?"

"And the longer we wait, the greater risk we run that someone will take offense that you didn't report Kris abandoned sooner. You could end up in trouble just for being in the wrong place at the wrong time."

Lori gazed down at the beautiful, fragile child in her arms. It was the *right* place. The *right* time. She gazed back up at him and willed the fear from her eyes. "Promise me one thing," she begged.

"I will if I can."

"Just promise me you'll give me until after Christmas."

He didn't say anything.

"That will give us three days."

"Three days to do what?"

"It will give me three days to find Kris's mother."

"We're much more likely to find her with the kind of help we'd get from governmental agencies," he offered.

"Promise me?"

He finally looked at her again. "And if we haven't found Kris's mom by then?"

Lori nodded. "I'll call the police or social services myself."

"Almost every office or agency is closed for the holiday weekend anyway," he said almost to himself.

"Okay. We won't take any action until after Christmas."

She forced herself to take a deep breath and meet his eyes. "You're right. You have no reason to trust me. I know you're—"

"We have—" he checked his watch "—about five and a half, six hours to remedy that." He grimaced. "I promised my mother I'd help her with some Christmas stuff this afternoon. I plan to go out there about three. Besides that, my calendar's clear."

Lori answered the question he implied. "I cleared my calendar for the week at 7:30 yesterday morning when I called in and said I wasn't coming to work." Lifting her hand from the baby's back, she tapped Kris lightly with her index finger. "She's my entire agenda until...until..."

"Good. Then we're all set." He stepped back abruptly, as if he'd also noticed he was too close. His smile widened and turned slightly wicked. "You want me to take her for a while so you can—" he gestured vaguely "—get dressed? Take a shower or something?"

Lori hadn't even thought about how she must look. From the chill she'd been unaware of until now, she knew her shabby and well-worn robe gaped open from top to bottom. The thin white gown beneath it would have done little to prevent his seeing anything that might be of any interest to him. Her skin tingled and tightened even as she told herself he wasn't the least bit interested.

His hand circled Kris, and Lori released the infant to his care, trying hard not to touch him as she did.

Not daring to look at him, she snatched the ends of her robe together and retied the belt. "I'll hurry," she promised, tugging at a short string of hair. She didn't even want to think about how it must look. Past experience told her it was standing on end all over her head.

"Take whatever time you need," he said, sounding amused. "In case you haven't figured it out, you don't always get much time to yourself with a baby around."

"I'm learning." Head bent, she started to leave them. She stopped by the door to the hall and looked back.

He'd stretched Kris out in front of him, precariously letting her hang in midair with one big hand behind her head while the other cradled her tiny, tiny butt. The position made Lori's breath catch. She reassured herself he knew what he was doing. He *wouldn't* chance dropping the baby even if he was watching Lori instead of what he was doing.

She knew she blushed furiously. "Don't do anything with her yet, will you?"

His appreciative stare turned into a questioning frown.

"I mean…doesn't she need a bath? Things like that? Will you wait for me? Not do anything until I can watch?"

He chuckled. "I'll do even better than that," he said. "I'll let you do it all while I stand around and give orders," he assured her with a slow, teasing wink. It was the sexiest wink she'd ever seen in her life. "Okay?"

How could she speak when she was so breathless? She had to nod. She hurried away as if the devil himself were at her heels.

CHAPTER FOUR

ANDY had had a very large weakness for babies as long as he could remember. His earliest memories involved his aunt from Colorado letting him sit beside her on the couch and hold his tiny cousins. Then his parents had produced his sisters and he'd rediscovered that babies were pretty special—until they grew out of babyhood and turned into "girls". He smiled to himself at those pleasant thoughts.

For now, this little girl was a sweetheart. And a mystery. Another of his greatest weaknesses.

"How are we going to solve your mystery?" he asked her. His voice drew her attention to his face. Smart, too. She was very alert considering her short time on the earth. He swayed her gently to and fro. "Who's your momma?"

The tiny little thing half smiled back at him. She had a tough road ahead of her.

"We really need to know," he told her.

She blinked, then yawned at him. Bored with the whole subject, she focused her attention on the ceiling light behind him.

They could check hospitals, see if there was a record of her birth. But Andy suspected that any mother who would put her baby on someone's doorstep would probably have had that baby alone. He jostled Kris lightly and watched her bat at the air with one fist. "Yeah. You'd better be a fighter," he told her. "You may need to be."

He glanced up to find Lori had returned. She wore a

nondescript sweat suit. Her short hair was still damp. She stood in the doorway with a wistful, left-out look on her face.

"You hurried," he commented, wanting to extend a hand to her, invite her in. He couldn't with his hands full of baby.

"I'm terrified I'm going to miss something." Lori's shrug accompanied a sheepish grimace. "I know it's silly." A demure blush made those green eyes more prominent than ever.

He wished he could give her some kind of guarantee that she wouldn't have to rush Kris's whole lifetime into three days. "I don't think it's silly at all," he said, and cleared his throat. "Come on. Let's give her a bath."

For the next hour, Andy played his version of child care expert and Lori flattered him by following every instruction without question. He wondered if his second-hand advice would get past his mother's close scrutiny.

As Lori finished dressing Kris, he found he liked having Lori think he was an expert. Maybe when his mother had started harassing him in earnest about settling down and getting married last summer, she was more perceptive than he'd given her credit for. Maybe he was closer to being ready for marriage and parenthood than he'd considered.

"What?" Lori's hand hovered over the last snap of the little sleeper. "Did I do something wrong?"

He realized he'd been scowling. "Not a thing," he reassured Lori quickly. "I was just thinking."

With only his slight assertion, Lori's intent, single-minded determination to do everything right returned. "If you'll take her—" she handed him the clean baby "—I'll run and wash this out." She held up Kris's one change of clothing. "At least it will have a chance to dry by the time we need it again."

Andy sniffed. "She doesn't smell like a baby."

Lori's horrified look redisplayed all her insecurities.

He repositioned Kris to move his spare hand to Lori's still-damp head. "You haven't done a thing wrong," he told her again, stroking and smoothing her dark hair. "The observation wasn't critical. She's not going to smell like a baby until we have some baby things. You know. Baby powder, lotion. It's time for you to go shopping."

"Now?"

He looked from her down to Kris, who was sucking on the back of one fist. Her eyes were seriously drooping. "She's ready to sleep. I bet she'll be out for a couple of hours. I'll stay and watch her. You may not get a better chance."

Lori looked strangely reluctant.

"I'll take notes if you'd like. You won't miss a thing."

Lori smiled sheepishly. "I'm being silly, aren't I?"

He let a grin answer her question. "Maybe we should both go," he suggested. "Take her with us."

Lori looked at him as though he'd gone crazy, her eyes growing wide. "You can't take a tiny baby out in...in this weather. Can you?" Her voice lifted uncertainly.

"You think families stay home all winter when they have a new baby?"

Her blank expression said that, yes, she had thought that. "But they surely have a coat or something warm to dress their babies in," she protested.

"That's why someone needs to go shopping," he pointed out. "Would you rather I go?"

Her grimace this time was tortured.

"You don't think I'm capable of shopping for a baby?"

Lori's sunny chuckle warmed him. "If *I* go," she commented dryly, "you'll have to help me figure out what we need since I have no idea. No. I'm torn between wanting to stay here and savor every second and wanting to pick out things for Kris myself."

Damn. Ninety-nine percent of the grown-up population might be able to take care of Kris's physical needs with more expertise, but no one in the world would love her any more than Lori.

Holding little Kris kept him from putting his arms around Lori as he suddenly wanted to. Instead, he offered her reassurance. "I'll think of something, Lori."

Her smile started small, quivered, then grew slowly until it lit up the room. "Then I'll go shopping."

"Good."

"Good." She looked over her shoulder as she turned away. "I'll get some paper. You can help me with my list." He'd never seen a woman so solemn, especially one about to set out on a shopping expedition. "I'll hurry," she promised as they completed it and she gathered her things.

"Don't hurry too much," he warned. "I'd hate to have to get my mom and sisters to give you remedial shopping lessons."

It coaxed out exactly the grin he'd hoped it would. "That shows what *you* know," she told him.

Not enough, Lori Warren. I don't know enough.

"But we'll change that later, won't we?" he told the sleeping baby after Lori left. "I suspect I know everything I *really* need to know," he added. "The important stuff."

As if she agreed, the corner of Kris's mouth turned up in her sleep. He went to lay her on Lori's bed.

Lori stopped at the discount store a couple of blocks from the apartment complex. It didn't take long to gather the essentials Andy had helped her put on her list.

Baby powder. Baby lotion. More diapers. Why hadn't she thought to ask Andy how much formula? Surely a case of the same brand that had come with Kris would get them through the next couple of days. Finally, she chose five or six of the tiny sleepers Kris seemed to go through with surprising regularity and a minuscule fluffy snowsuit. She buried her nose in it, testing its warmth. It felt soft and comforting. Kris would like it.

Lori worked her way down the baby aisle, reading packages, amazed at the array of items and gadgets made "especially for baby". Lori found herself throwing in a few pairs of the tiniest, most precious little socks she'd ever seen. One of this, one of that. She threw various items into her cart, cautioning herself not to get too carried away.

Until she knew what was going to happen, there wasn't much point in spending a lot on things like baby beds. Lori took one look at the price tag dangling from the end of a bassinet and turned away.

A Christmas display at the end of the baby aisle stopped her short. A giant stocking, about the same size as Kris, was lettered Baby's First Christmas. Kris's whole little body would fit neatly inside it, but its real purpose was obvious. A sample was stuffed to the brim and overflowing, showing a doting mom and dad how to spend all their money filling it. A rattle, some plastic baby blocks and a fluffy panda had spilled out amid red and green and gold and silver tinsel. Beside that, a tiny red velvet dress, trimmed in soft white lace with a holly-colored ribbon, lay as though it had been taken from a closet, then tossed aside for a moment.

In the background, Christmas music played. Frazzled shoppers scurried about with nary a "joyful and triumphant'' expression on a single face. But the feeling was there, in the air, throughout the store…in Lori Warren, she realized with a start.

As sneakily as some extremely contagious disease, the highly touted, much discussed Christmas spirit had mysteriously attacked her.

A little way down from Lori, a tired-looking young woman frowned at a caged stuffed raccoon in a display in the center of the aisle. She absentmindedly stroked the neck of the huge giraffe standing on the floor beside the ''zoo''. The woman's eyes lost their dazed look for a moment. A smile flitted across her face as she realized what she'd been petting. She picked him up, smiled directly into his face and nestled the giraffe lovingly between her own box of newborn-size disposable diapers and some rolls of wrapping paper.

Just like *that* woman's baby, Kris was going to have a wonderful Christmas, Lori decided, stiffening her back. She wasn't going to meet her friends in Colorado. She wouldn't have those expenses on her charge card; a few things for Kris wouldn't sink her.

The tiny baby wouldn't remember her first Christmas but Lori suddenly didn't care. *She* would. Whatever happened, Lori would remember this Christmas always, whether Kris did or not.

It was going to be very special.

Andy opened the door of her apartment while she was still fumbling with her key. ''You must have bought the store out.''

''I tried,'' she admitted, peering around her armload of packages. ''And you were worried about my shopping skills,'' she mocked him.

He took the bag blocking her view, placed it on the

end of the couch and reached for the rest. "Here. Let me take those. You can hang up your coat."

"There's more," she admitted sheepishly.

His eyebrows rose.

"You've been busy," she said, noting the straightened room. No scattered clothes or dirty dishes and the trash had been cleared; it was almost back to the neatly cluttered room it had been before Kris had invaded her life.

He shrugged. "Just wanted to help."

"Thanks." She looked up at him, once again bemused by his many facets. "How's Kris?"

"Still asleep."

She shook her head, suddenly aware of how weary she was. Shopping combined with a lack of sleep the night before didn't exactly make her feel sharp. Why hadn't Kris slept this long a stretch for her? She angled her head at him. "I hope you're going to tell me *this* secret."

He winked. "Would you believe, my restful presence?"

"Good. You'll stay tonight?" She said it without thinking, but the air was suddenly charged with a tension she couldn't begin to think about. Her gaze seem locked on his mouth.

"Maybe," he said softly, his white teeth showing seductively from between his mesmerizing lips. "If you ask me very nicely."

Her heart stopped for a second. "I...I guess I'm out of luck. I don't do nice. I'll be right back." She ducked out and hurried back down to her car, forestalling his offer of assistance. Unloading her treasures took three more trips and at least she had an excuse for feeling as if she couldn't catch her breath.

By the time Andy helped her out of her coat, the order

he'd brought to her living room had returned to chaos. It looked as if a store had relocated there.

"You sure you got everything you need?" Andy teased, pulling a stuffed panda from the closest sack.

She snatched the bag away from him, achingly aware that he'd realize just how excessive she'd been if he saw the aftershave and the eye-catching necktie. He'd know *those* couldn't be for Kris.

"I...let me do that." She felt her face flush as he gazed at her. "I...I...got some Christmas things," she explained.

He scrutinized her with a smile. "And that embarrasses you?"

"A little," she admitted, avoiding his eyes. "I got carried away. Just like you warned me not to."

He took the package from between them and returned it to the coffee table. "Lori..."

She gazed up at him. His dark eyes searched her face. "Yes?"

He laid his warm hand against her winter-cold cheek. "I don't want you to..." His voice suddenly became gruff.

"Yes?" Her own voice sounded husky to her ears.

"Don't invest too much in this child. And I don't mean money," he added with an edge.

She searched for words, then abruptly shook her head, pulling herself loose from him, moving away. "I haven't told you some things."

"Like?"

"Like I may have lost my job."

"You may have? What do you mean, you *may* have?"

"Well..." She shrugged. "When I called in and said I wasn't coming in yesterday—my last day before the holidays—my new boss fired me."

"So you *don't* have a job."

She lifted a shoulder again. "Except my new boss is…well…new. The top spot at the convention and visitors' bureau is a political appointment. He's still a bit at a loss. Firing me was panic talking. He had to make an important presentation on his own, one he wasn't looking forward to anyway. I'm sure it went well. I figure by the time I'm due back from vacation, he'll have reconsidered."

"You're indispensable?" His good-humored gaze came to rest on her lips.

They were suddenly very dry and she wet the lower one with a cautious dip of her tongue. "I love what I do and I'm very good at it," she said, borrowing his phrase of the day before. "Which is part of my boss's problem."

"How so?"

"I should have had the job he was appointed to. He knows it. He has attacks of paranoia from time to time."

"He thinks you missed the meeting to sabotage him?"

"I suspect so." Lori nodded and glanced toward the hall leading to the bedroom where Andy had put Kris to sleep. "Deep down, he knows better. I've never been resentful. *And*," she emphasized, "it's a city job. It doesn't pay as well as it could. It won't be easy to replace me." She turned her attention back to Andy. "Besides, I'll be able to tell him about Kris by the time I'm due back to work. I just couldn't tell him when I called, so he naturally wasn't very understanding."

Andy frowned at her. "I have a feeling there was a point to this. Have I missed it?"

She couldn't help grinning. "You told me not to invest too much." She raised a hand. "I know you weren't talking about money, but it reminded me that I spent more on all of this than I should have, especially given the situation."

"You're probably right," he said, raising an eyebrow at all the sacks of merchandise scattered around them.

"I wanted you to know I'm not really worried about my job. Then I realized you didn't know I'd lost it in the first place and it may affect things with...with Kris and whether I can keep her or not. As my lawyer, I thought you should know."

"If you have a job," he reminded her wryly.

"If I have a job," she conceded.

"What exactly do you do anyway, Lori?"

"I'm the director of association sales for Kansas City."

"So what *exactly* do you do?" Andy asked again with that broad grin, the one that seemed too personal, the one that made her feel like a mass of metal shavings being pulled toward a powerful magnet. "It sounds important."

Looking around her at the clutter of bags, she used them as a distraction. "I sell the city and everything it has to offer to associations that are looking for a place to hold business meetings or conventions." She began pulling the baby necessities out of the various sacks and piling them on the coffee table.

"You enjoy it?"

"It's a great job. I meet a lot of fascinating people," she responded. "I get to travel a bit. Wine and dine VIPs at Kansas City's most trendy, interesting places I couldn't afford myself without the expense account. See the sights." She transferred Christmas gifts and wrapping supplies to several bags to take to her bedroom. "I like it."

"If your boss doesn't rehire you, will you have trouble finding something else?"

She shook her head. "One of the best hotels in the city has been bugging me to go to work for them in their sales department for the past year and a half. It would pay better because I'd get commissions. That's what I wanted you to know. I'm not worried. I *can* take care of Kris. Financially anyway," she assured him with a smile. "I can make a living, even if it isn't an overly extravagant one."

"Have you considered that it might be handy to have two parents around to raise a baby, Lori?"

The question stilled her for a moment as a vision flashed through her mind. His head bent next to hers as he helped her bathe the baby this morning. It was a vivid image. The unplanned partnership they'd formed in such a short period of time must surely be a taste of what marriage and having a family must be. But that wasn't what he meant at all.

His second softly spoken question confirmed that. "Have you considered what it will be like to raise a child on your own? Assuming you can adopt her, of course."

"I haven't had time to think that far ahead," she admitted. She dodged the mess she hadn't cleared, just rearranged, to take a couple of sacks to the bedroom.

"Have you considered, Lori," Andy continued when she reappeared, "that maybe *you'd* be better off if we just called in the authorities and let—"

"How can you possibly think that?" She'd been reaching for more shopping bags. Instead, her hands fisted and landed on her hips.

"You're meant to be someone's mother, Lori. I can see that."

Lori forced herself not to wince.

"But have you thought that maybe it would be easier

the traditional way?'' he continued. ''Find a nice husband, have a kid every couple of years?''

''That's what *you* want.''

''But not you?''

She refused to let him see the way this conversation affected her. She studied the bags around her intently. ''I doubt I'll get married,'' she said lightly.

''You have something against the state of holy matrimony?''

''Let's just say it's never been in my plans.''

''You're a beautiful, caring woman, Lori.''

She cast a startled glance at him.

''Why wouldn't marriage be in your plans eventually?'' One corner of his mouth turned up, revealing a tiny little crease in his cheek that could be a dimple. ''I can't believe you don't expect anyone to ask.''

''Sure,'' she said, working hard at remaining nonchalant. ''I beat men off with a stick daily.''

''Why does that not surprise me?'' he said too seriously, despite his smile.

''What's wrong with you if you're so all-fired hot on the subject? Why aren't you enjoying that blissful state?''

Her turning the tables on him took him by amused surprise. His brown eyes warmed with admiration and the dimple sneaked out again.

She'd always had a thing for dimples.

''I'm waiting for someone who'll make me think kids and fatherhood and apple-pie thoughts,'' he drawled, obviously pleased with his answer. His gaze held steady on her. ''Like I said. I plan to marry someday. But don't think you're getting off that lightly.'' He shook his head. ''Anyone ever tell you that you're terrific at changing the subject? I don't think we've finished one conversation yet. This one, we finish. Why don't you plan to get married, Lori?''

Because I can't marry someone like you. The thought crystallized so quickly, so unexpectedly, it stunned her. She blessed herself for not saying it aloud.

She knew she turned somber. Try as she might, she couldn't seem to bring back the carefree teasing tone of a moment before. ''I don't form those kinds of relationships easily.''

''What do you mean?''

''Close relationships. I don't get close to people. I think that's a prerequisite if you plan to marry someone.'' She gave him the best replica of a smile she could muster. ''You know this morning when you asked where my friends were? Why I didn't turn to them?''

He nodded, but the almost imperceptible little lines between his brows grew deep.

''I don't have any. Not the kind you were talking about anyway,'' she added when he started to protest. ''Please. Don't look so troubled. It's not a bad thing. It's just a fact.''

''How can you say that?''

''What? That it's not bad? Or that I don't have friends?''

''Either.'' His horror tainted every feature.

''Look. I have a very full, very satisfying life. I have friends at work. We do things together.'' She made a broad, sweeping gesture. ''I'm friendly with all my neighbors. I have friends from college that I see several times a year.''

''You don't make friends easily? Look at the way you've charmed and practically turned me into your slave.''

''I had to pay you,'' Lori protested, aware as she did that she *had* been taking advantage of him. She giggled.

"You didn't know when you forced me to hire you that I would expect your undivided attention and full-time domestic services, did you?"

"No," he said dryly, sharing her amusement with a rueful smile.

"I...I'm sorry. I didn't mean to turn you into a baby-sitter and...and...household help."

"I haven't done a thing I didn't want to." Andy's gaze seared Lori's face. "I have a feeling the lack of retainer wouldn't have made a bit of difference. Until we get this all straightened out, you may as well plan on me being around. Whether you like it or not."

"But you—"

He pressed a long, sensuous finger over her lips. "Whether you like it or not," he repeated.

The thank-you she mouthed was heartfelt. "See? You just proved my point." She lifted one shoulder and flippantly remarked, "My life isn't bad. I *do* have people when I need them. I have a social life. I have a job I love...."

"But no *close* friends?" He was obviously trying hard to understand.

"I suppose it depends on what you call close. I don't tell all my secrets to anyone, if that's what you mean. I don't have any particular friend I feel I absolutely must talk to each day." She smiled at him brightly. "I'll admit I feel lonely occasionally, but doesn't everyone? Don't you? Truly, I'm content with my life."

It was almost amusing. She'd rendered the handsome lawyer speechless. She suspected the condition might be a rarity.

"Right now," she admitted, feeling almost impish, "*you* know more of my 'secrets' than anyone else I know. Except maybe my sister," she added as an afterthought.

"You have a sister?" He gave her a confused scowl.

"A foster sister," she clarified. "We lived in the same home a couple of years. We were fifteen and sixteen when we got there and we became sort of close."

"Why didn't you call *her* when you found Kris?"

"She lives in a little town in Connecticut. She moved there when she got married two years ago. We keep in touch," she added, "but we aren't as close as we used to be." She sighed. "I suppose that's normal. She has a husband. She's going to have a baby next April, so I'm going to be an aunt."

Another thought dawned on her. "Wouldn't it be nice if Sharon's baby...? That's my foster sister," she inserted, needlessly, she realized when he nodded. "Wouldn't it be nice if Sharon's baby had a cousin to grow up with?"

"Lori..." Andy's voice held a sharp warning.

"No." She held up a hand. "Don't say it. I'm not getting my hopes up. I've lived too long to expect miracles. I know I may not get to keep her," she managed to whisper. "And I know you're right, but..."

Andy, who'd been prowling the room the past few minutes, stopped in front of her. "But," he urged when she didn't go on.

"My head keeps listening to your advice," she murmured, looking down at the cranberry-colored polish on her fingertips. She rubbed at the smooth surface of one fingernail with her thumb. "But my heart doesn't seem to care what you say. Or what I *think*, for that matter."

His hand moved to her shoulder.

"I know you're afraid we won't be able to find a way for me to keep her..."

She felt his nod of agreement more than saw it.

"But sometimes..." She glanced directly up at him.

"Have you ever just felt, deep in your soul, that something was right?"

His concern deepened his frown. "You mean that all of this will work out?"

"No, I'm not saying that. I accept that you may not find a way for me to keep her," she said.

His hand tightened. It felt warm, comforting, even through the heavy sweatshirt. "Lori, I will try—"

"I know you'll do your very best. What I mean is…" She paused. "Don't get me wrong. I want to keep Kris more than anything I've ever wanted in my life." Her hands flattened against his solid chest, imploring him to understand. She couldn't hide the tears forming in her eyes this time. She didn't try to. "This baby is here—with me—for a reason," she told him earnestly. "Deep in my soul, I know it." She dabbed at the dampness at the corner of her eyes and stood up straighter, dropping her hands to her sides. "In the meantime, I'm going to give her the best Christmas a tiny baby could have."

He winced. "Lori, she won't ever remem—"

"I *know* she won't remember." Her voice broke and came back a whisper. "But maybe it will be there, in the back of her mind. Maybe she won't dread holidays for the rest of her life."

Andy closed his eyes, then opened them to stare at a spot on the other side of the room, somewhere above her head.

"And I'm going to love her so hard she can feel it, even if she doesn't know what it is and even if it's just for a few days. And I'm going to do my darnedest to take good care of her, however long I have her." Smiling gently at the man who was looking at her with so much compassion she was certain he could make her heart burst with a word, she reiterated, "Whatever happens, it's right. I know it is."

"Don't sell me short, Lori. I'm going to do everything in my power to help you," he said intently. "And don't sell yourself short, either. There's nothing wrong— sometimes it even helps—with expecting the best."

She sighed and reminded herself that her growing admiration for Andy had nothing to do with him personally. It was the situation. It was hero worship. Falling for him would be a hopeless disaster, much worse than getting too attached to Kris. At least with Kris, there was a *chance* she could keep her.

So she did the only thing she could really do about Andy. "I thank you, Andrew McAllister, from the bottom of my heart," she finished with passion, rising on tiptoes to place an uninvited kiss on his whisker-roughened cheek, "for whatever you can do to help."

CHAPTER FIVE

ANDY stomped downstairs when he left Lori's apartment an hour later. "For whatever I can do to help," he muttered as he slammed his car door harder than he intended. He'd never felt so frustrated in his life.

He couldn't think of a thing to do for her, but she'd thanked him anyway. He couldn't even hold her and offer her the physical comfort he'd given client after client in the past. Somehow this was different. The first time he'd wanted to, he'd been holding Kris. The second time he hadn't dared. He hadn't been feeling the least bit lawyerly and he wouldn't have wanted to stop with a simple hug. He'd had an incredibly powerful urge to kiss her until she couldn't see straight, then make love to her until she couldn't think of anything else.

Instead, he'd offered empty platitudes.

His mother always said God knew what He was doing, even if we couldn't always figure it out. The baby was with Lori Warren so *her* childhood wounds could heal. That was obvious. Pouring out all that love Lori'd been storing up and hoarding for years was healing her.

After her impassioned speech, she'd set about putting together a small plastic Christmas tree she'd brought home in a box.

She should have a *real* tree. A big tree.

He'd strung the lights for her, then held the baby while she'd decorated the tree that barely reached his eye level—and he was six foot two—even after setting it on an end table.

He'd watched her open the cellophane-covered boxes

of shiny, brand-new ornaments and thought of the big battered boxes his mother made someone carry down from the attic year after year.

Lori's smile came and went while she'd carefully spaced the impersonal, nondescript, brightly colored balls. He couldn't help but compare them with his mother's unmatched bedraggled ones. Every decoration told a story. They were things he, his sisters, family and friends had made or contributed over the years. Some of the most sentimental things had been passed down through several generations.

He'd listened to Lori's oohs and aahs as she stepped back to admire her handiwork and been speechless when she'd asked his opinion. Andy didn't think he'd ever be able to look at another Christmas tree without thinking of the expression that had cloaked Lori's face when she'd finally taken the baby and asked him to flick on the lights.

"For my first tree, I didn't do so badly, did I?" she had asked and thanked him again when he said it looked great.

"Thanks for whatever I can do," he grumbled now. "And I can't seem to *do* a damn thing."

If God had sent him to help Lori, he wished to high heaven the Man would give him a clue how. What would happen if he didn't come up with some legal fix? he wondered as he pulled into the short driveway of his parents' home.

"My gracious! What's the matter?" Veronica asked as she opened the back door to him. "You look like a thundercloud."

"I *feel* like a thundercloud," Andy told her.

She brushed his cheek with a kiss and held her hand out for his coat. "What's wrong?"

"My new case. The one I was telling you about," he muttered.

"You told me virtually nothing," his mother said dryly, drawing him into the warm, spice-scented kitchen.

He sniffed the air. "You've been making gingerbread men."

"Gingerbread toy soldiers," she corrected, and joined him in appreciative deep breathing. Her expression turned reprimanding as she slapped at his hand. "Those are for Michael and Kevin. They'll be thrilled with them."

"I would be thrilled with one, too," Andy remarked, smiling.

She shook her head warningly. "Here, have this instead." Veronica poured him a mug of homemade eggnog, adding a liberal dash of rum. "What's the problem with your new case?" Her pale blue eyes darkened, grew wider, then darkened again as he told her about Lori and little Kris. "Oh, my," she said when he was finally through.

"What does 'oh, my' mean?"

"Come on," she said, rising from the place she'd taken across from him at the kitchen table. "Let's go hang greenery."

"You aren't going to comment?" Andy asked as he followed her.

"I suspect you wouldn't like a single thing I have to say." Her lips closed primly as she handed him one end of an evergreen swag.

"Try me," he suggested after a moment. He picked up the stapler and started up the ladder.

"For one thing, I don't think it sounds like you have any business representing this girl," she said.

She was right. He wasn't going to particularly like

what she had to say if her first comment was anything
to go by. "Oh?"

"This sounds like the kind of thing that could turn
into a huge media event. A baby left on a doorstep at
Christmas? With that judicial nomination hanging in the
balance..." She left him to finish the thought himself.

He let a section of greenery drape from the ceiling,
down about a foot on the wall, then up again. "I don't
have a lot to lose. I told you how the dinner at the governor's went. He's pretty much written me off anyway."
He fastened that loop and a second with staples, then
started down so he could move the ladder. "If I handle
it right, it could bring very positive publicity. I haven't
noticed he's averse to good publicity."

Veronica played out a bit more of the greenery. "And
if it doesn't turn out well? If it's bad publicity?"

"How can a baby left on a doorstep at Christmastime
be bad publicity?" His mother was silent too long. He
stopped beside her before he headed up the ladder again.

"It could be bad publicity however it turns out," she
said.

He stapled the next swag with a little more energy
than necessary. "You want to explain that for me?" he
asked.

"Well," she started, handing him another end of evergreen rope, "if you try this in the court of public opinion—as I'm sure you've considered—there will be people who want your friend to keep the child. But there
will also be people coming out of the woodwork who
want to adopt the baby." She paused. "Some of them
will be much more suited while many people will feel
your friend isn't appropriate at all. It'll be kind of like
the Biblical Solomon thing. The governor will stay as
far away from that kind of controversy as possible. And
he'll think you're a fool for getting involved, too." She

gave Andy a censoring look at his one-word expletive. "That kind of language won't get you a judicial appointment," she warned primly.

"And that's the problem," he said. "If I was already a judge, I could take care of this. Why are judges the only ones in the child welfare system allowed to use common sense?"

He was at the bottom of the ladder again. His mother patted his arm. "If you're so certain a judge would use common sense, why didn't you immediately file a petition for custody on your client's behalf?"

He didn't like his mother's question. She knew it.

"Am I right in feeling you believe the judge is going to immediately put that child in the custody of the state? You don't have a single solitary idea about how to stop that from happening?"

"It's wrong," he protested. "Lori's so right for that child."

"And that's the other problem," his mother said.

He eyed her skeptically as he moved the ladder, then started up it again. "You aren't going to be happy until you tell me your other problems with all this," he told her. "You may as well finish."

She cleared her throat. "You don't exactly sound like an uninterested party."

"What's that supposed to mean?" He didn't dare look at her. He looped the end of the evergreen rope over the ladder and made his way down.

"You should turn this case over to Melanie or your father."

He propped his hands on his jean-clad hips. "Why?"

"See? You're getting defensive. If this was a normal case, you wouldn't be." As much as he loved his mother, sometimes he hated her smug declarations.

"You can't pay attention to the legal details if you can only see the big picture."

"Make up your mind, Mom. A minute ago, you were more or less agreeing with me that judges should make decisions based on common sense. That's the big picture, isn't it? Now, you're worried about the details? You can't have it both ways."

"There's a big difference in having an intensity for what you're doing and having an intensity for *who* you are doing it for. I think it's called a conflict of interest."

"And what makes you think—"

"Can you name a single other client you baby-sit for?"

Andy threw up his hands. "I told you, Lori has no idea what she's doing. She can't help it. She hasn't—"

"Which would indicate to most people that the first course of action should be calling in someone who *does* know what they are doing. You're playing with your career, Andrew. And with a child's life."

"Not really." He resented feeling obligated to defend his actions or his rationale. He felt like a thirteen-year-old again. For once, Veronica didn't know what she was talking about. "We're going to figure out whose child it is," he said. "Pursue private adoption."

"Oh. You'll help convince some uncaring, irresponsible mother to give her child to a woman who has no business having her, either."

He started to protest, then realized she was playing devil's advocate. He sighed and tried a new tactic. "What have you always said a child needs more than anything, Mom?"

Veronica didn't even hesitate. "Love."

"Lori needs a how-to-care-for-your-baby book. No doubt about it. But if you'd only seen her with—"

"I'd love to. Bring them here for Christmas," his mother interrupted.

Veronica's suggestion stunned Andy and shut him up. Why hadn't he thought of it? Where else in the world could Kris get the kind of loving—and experienced—care she deserved? Lori would watch and learn and soak up everything she needed to know. He felt a smile spreading.

And seeing was believing. If he brought Lori home, his mother, his father, his sisters, the whole family would see what he had seen. They'd be lining up to be character witnesses, to testify as to Lori's fitness to be Kris's guardian. Whatever else his family was, they were well-known and highly respected in the judicial system in this county.

And the Christmas that would be happening at *this* house was exactly the kind of Christmas Lori should experience.

But what if it *was* only a one-time thing in her life?

No. She'd have others, once she had a holiday like the warm, wonderful one his mother always managed to provide. Lori would set up housekeeping herself someday, have a couple of kids. She'd have Christmases *her* own children would treasure.

He grabbed his mother and kissed her on the end of her squat little nose. "Thanks, Mom."

She looked at him suspiciously for a second. "Glad to be useful," she finally said. "And of course, it will make handing the case over to Melanie a smoother transition for both you and…"

"Lori," he supplied. He couldn't decide if he felt a niggling irritation because she couldn't remember Lori's name or if it stemmed from her suggestion that he should hand the case over to Melanie. "We'll see." He glanced at his watch, already impatient to get back to Lori's

apartment and find out what was happening at that end.
"Come on. Let's finish getting this stuff hung."

Lori was trying hard not to panic as she tried to make a
list of names of who Kris's mother might be. The very
fact that the baby's mother had left Kris with Lori ought
to be some clue. Who would choose her? And why?

"I *do* know her," she reassured herself before groan-
ing and burying her face in her hands. She'd told Andy
she would be able to figure it out. Yesterday, she'd felt
so certain. Today, she wondered if Andy was right. The
mother had only brought her up to the third floor of the
apartment building to protect her from the cold blasts
that often accompanied people into the building. And
Lori's was the first apartment door on this floor.

When the doorbell rang, she was almost thankful for
the interruption, especially since the sound didn't wake
Kris. She let Andy in and hushed him with a finger over
her lips.

"She's still asleep?" he asked aloud.

"Yes," she mouthed.

"Babies don't need total quiet when they sleep,
Lori," he told her as she held out a hand for his coat.
"Start as you mean to go or you'll end up running
around shushing people your whole life," he warned.

His voice sounded as loud as thunder and Kris's cry
from the bedroom had Lori's eyes narrowing at him.
"Thanks for the advice," she said wryly.

He lifted his shoulders in an apologetic hey-I-didn't-
do-anything shrug as she hung his coat in the closet.
"Just wait until you have another one," he warned
again. "You going to knock one out so the other can
sleep?"

She didn't bother showing him her grimace. "I don't
think I'll waste a lot of time worrying about it."

"You want her to sleep tonight, don't you?" He ambled behind her as she went toward the bedroom.

"Oh, yes," she pleaded.

"Then it's time she woke anyway."

He propped himself against the door frame as Lori picked up Kris, checking her diaper. She grabbed a disposable from the box she'd set next to the bed. She was pleased with how efficient she was getting at this. She smugly laid the baby back down over the diaper.

"Did you have a nice nap, sweetie?" she crooned, feeling a little self-conscious. No matter how she tried otherwise, no matter who was watching, she couldn't seem to talk to Kris without using a singsongy voice. She consoled herself with the thought that Andy talked to Kris the same silly way.

"Did *you* get a nap?" he asked as she rearranged Kris's clothes.

She shook her head. "I tried but my mind was racing. I gave up after a few minutes." Weariness must be a permanent state when you had a baby around, she decided. Andy's shoulder looked like an inviting place to rest as she started around him.

He must have read her mind. He casually swung an arm around her shoulders, pulling her head lightly against him as they strolled down the narrow hall together. She smiled up at him automatically when they reached the end of it.

They both stopped. His gaze dropped from her eyes to her mouth. Lori's mind felt as empty as a balloon. The smile he usually wore was transformed into something tense. She watched, fascinated, as the muscle in his jaw rippled. His hand lifted to cup her upper arm, and unexpected but pleasant sensations skidded up her shoulder, down her neck.

They might have been frozen there forever if Kris hadn't kicked and broken the spell.

"She's hungry," Lori said unnecessarily and somehow managed to move on.

Andy held out his arms for Kris as soon as they reached the kitchen. Somehow, Lori avoided touching him as she handed Kris over. He helped in the effort by some unspoken agreement, but they shouldn't have bothered. Trying to stay away from him only increased Lori's tingling awareness of him. Knowing his hands were only centimeters away from hers was as distracting as the actual contact would have been.

Lori turned to get a bottle out of the refrigerator. "I'm getting quite good at this routine, don't you think?" she asked for something to say.

"I think you're—" His face clouded as he broke off.

She shot him an uncomprehending frown and turned on the microwave to heat the bowl of water that was fast becoming a permanent fixture in there. She didn't understand what was going on between them. She crossed her arms self-consciously and leaned back against the counter to wait for the water to boil so she could warm the bottle in it.

He shook his head as if he was annoyed with himself and a stiff, unnatural smile returned. He jiggled Kris as she began to fuss.

The microwave dinged and Lori thankfully retrieved the bowl and set the cold bottle in it.

"As soon as she's fed, why don't we get out of here for a while?" he suggested out of the blue.

"What?"

"She has a warm little snowsuit now," he reminded her. "You surely want her to have a chance to wear it."

"But—"

"I still need to finish my Christmas shopping," he explained. "I'd love it if you'd help."

Lori laughed. "Don't you sound just like a man." She'd finished her new boss's Christmas shopping for him, she explained when Andy frowned. She'd offered when her boss had been stewing about the last couple of presents he had to buy. She was certain he would be pleased with his wife's reaction to her choice. That was one reason she felt confident the boss would be feeling more charitable to her after Christmas.

"An effort to get on his good side?"

Lori let a noncommittal smile answer the question. "It was also a great excuse to get out of the office awhile." She looked back at Kris. "But do you think—"

"If Kris gives us the slightest hint she isn't enjoying her first evening out," he responded quickly, anticipating her next protest, "we'll come home immediately. Besides," he continued with the same glint in his eyes, "I have it on good authority that half the fun of having kids is showing them off. Wouldn't you like to show off Kris?"

The idea appealed to Lori a lot. "On whose good authority?"

"A couple of sisters and a very proud grandmother," he answered.

Getting out with Andy and taking Kris sounded like a huge adventure. If he thought it was okay to take Kris out, it must be.

"Good." He sensed her acquiescence before she said it. "You get ready while I feed her, then I'll run down and change," he suggested as she tested the bottle's contents on her wrist.

She felt suddenly lighthearted. "What? You don't want to go with me looking like this?" she asked, handing over the bottle and indicating her worn sweat suit at the same time.

He concentrated on getting the baby started on her dinner before he glanced up. His gaze lingered on her face, then grazed her body. The tension that had infused the atmosphere was back. "It isn't nearly as interesting as those cute little shorts you wear down in the workout room," he said dryly, the hint of a dimple sneaking out again. "But if that's what you'd like to wear…"

He *had* noticed her when they'd met in the complex's exercise facility in the basement of the clubhouse. "I'll change," she said after one speechless moment.

Andy leisurely carried Kris to the armchair in the living room and sat down.

Lori finally found her legs and scurried to her room.

As Kris ate, Andy wondered if Lori volunteered to shop for her boss for another reason she hadn't mentioned. When you were pretty much alone, like Lori was, whom did you buy Christmas gifts for? What kind of hell would Christmas be without family and friends? No wonder she'd gone to extremes for a baby who couldn't unwrap or appreciate a single gift.

After she finished, Kris watched him from the antiquated baby seat he'd wedged firmly against the arm of the couch. Andy talked softly to her as he took her empty bottle into the kitchen and rinsed it, then began packing the things Kris might need in a book bag Lori had supplied.

Kris had fallen asleep sucking on her fist by the time Lori reappeared.

She had changed into stylishly faded jeans and a sweater decorated like a giant Christmas present. The bow across the middle caressed her curves, hinting at joy on Christmas morning. He stood for a moment, breathless with the desire to unwrap her, to mold her against him to see if she fitted as perfectly as he imagined she would.

Lori babbled on while she checked what he had put in the bag. Andy was aware of what she was saying as she chattered, but his thoughts were on a different level.

Veronica McAllister had seen it. No wonder he'd willingly gone from lawyer to baby-sitter without thought, taken on Lori's problems as if they were his own. Somehow, in the past twenty-four hours, he'd become totally mesmerized with a waif who needed him as much as Kris needed her.

Her short brown hair softly framed her face and left her long neck bare and inviting. A curl shaped itself around her ear and kissed at the candy-cane earrings she'd put on. He wanted to explore the same territory with kisses of his own. Feel her heartbeat there. Gauge her reaction.

His reaction to her was purely chemical. Had to be. But as her attorney, he couldn't prove or disprove the theory one way or the other.

"Should I change her clothes?" Lori was asking.

"Do you want to?" he managed.

She nodded, smiling sheepishly. "If I'm going to show her off…"

He loved that look—trepidation at being caught treating Kris like a new toy mixed with the excitement at doing exactly that. "Then I think you should."

He watched as she bent to lift the sleeping infant. No one would mistake the adoration in Lori's eyes and the gentle handling for something that would wear off. Kris would never need to worry that Lori would tire of her. For a moment, he felt a twinge of jealousy.

"But save the little Christmas thing," he called after them as Lori started purposefully down the hall. She stopped and looked back at him. "One of the warmer things, don't you think?"

Lori's initial disappointment changed quickly to a look of gratitude. "You think of everything," she said with renewed admiration, leaving him feeling almost guilty. That bit of guidance had nothing to do with practicalities and everything to do with vanity. He looked forward to showing them both off himself when he took them home. He wanted Kris to look well cared for and pampered. He wanted Lori to have the credit.

The fresh-out-of-the-box plastic tree in the corner mocked him. It pretended to be a Christmas tree. Lori was playing mommy, complete with a real, live doll. He was pretending to be an attorney who could do some legal hocus-pocus and make everything all right. The thoughts and wishes he had right now had nothing to do with legalities.

He didn't want to think what would happen when playtime was over.

CHAPTER SIX

THE next hour flew by quickly.

Andy's first stop was at a huge baby store where he bought a combination car seat/carrier/infant seat for Kris's Christmas present. Compared to the old-fashioned infant carrier Kris had arrived in, this one looked like something found in a space shuttle. He insisted they use it now.

"It isn't Christmas yet," Lori pointed out.

"You got plenty of things for her to unwrap," he teased as he attached the seat firmly in the back of his car with the seat belt. "I'll feel a lot better about driving around town with her this way." Kris, who had been awake since Lori changed her clothes, immediately fell asleep in the seat once they were on the road again. "She likes it," he said smugly.

Lori decided Andy's idea of Christmas shopping was to buy everything he saw. Forty-five minutes later, he reviewed the list he'd retrieved when he'd stopped at his apartment and pronounced his Christmas shopping finished.

"Let's get out of here," he said as they left yet another shop in the mall. "This place is turning into a zoo."

They made one more stop at the booth where volunteers were wrapping presents to raise money for a charitable cause.

"They'll have them ready to pick up any time after nine-thirty," he said, glancing at his watch. "That gives us time for dinner." Andy walked in front of Lori and

Kris, parting the crowd of shoppers with his broad shoulders.

He stopped at the main mall entrance and set his packages down so he could help her fold the blanket around Kris's pastel yellow snowsuit.

"Kris has been really good," Lori said with irrepressible pride. "But don't you think we might be pushing our luck to take her somewhere public for dinner?"

"Oh ye of little faith," he said, tapping a long, gloved finger against the side of her nose. "She's a good baby. Don't you want to give her a chance to show you how good?"

Lori nodded and felt her heart swell with pride. Kris *was* a good baby. She'd known it but she did need his confirmation.

He took the baby from her so she could refasten her own coat. Then telling her, "Wait a second, I have a great idea," he gave the baby back and left them standing near the entrance. He went to the bank of phones lining the center of the walkway. Kris was straining against the blanket swaddling her by the time he returned. "All set," he announced, then opened the door to escort them out into the night.

Diamond-bright stars hung lower than usual, as if they'd frozen just out of arm's reach in the cold sky. The night felt magic. Their feet crunched in the slush that was in the process of refreezing.

Andy's hand rested on Lori's waist as he steered her around a tire-sculpted patch of ice. The simple gesture made her feel warm, protected.

Kris whimpered softly as Andy pulled his seat forward and strapped her into the infant seat. The cry was getting impatient by the time he started the car. Lori reached back between the seats to pat her, preparing to argue that maybe they should return to the apartment. But by the time they pulled out of the immense parking lot and before Lori could get a word out, Kris fell asleep again.

Andy winked as if he knew what she'd been thinking and hummed a few bars of Handel's *Messiah* along with the CD player. He turned the luxury sedan away from the mall with its tentacles of strip shopping centers and restaurants, away from the direction of the apartment complex, farther out toward the suburbs.

"Where—"

Andy held up his hand, obviously not planning on telling her their destination. "You'll see."

Lori had to admit she was intrigued when he turned into an exclusive upscale development marked by a native-stone entry...until it occurred to her that he might be taking her to his parents' home. Hadn't he said they only lived about twenty minutes from the apartment complex? The telephone call. He'd called home.

"Andy, I don't—"

"You'll like where I'm taking you to dinner," he promised.

Another turn into a cul-de-sac lined with extravagant houses in various stages of completion and Andy pulled into one of the wide driveways. This huge house looked more finished than most of the surrounding ones, but there were no curtains or lights. The windows were shimmering black accents in the gray native-stone exterior.

"Give me a few minutes," he ordered before she could ask any questions. Putting the car into Park, he left the engine idling and heater running as he opened his door.

The "Hallelujah Chorus" played as she watched him stroll up the snow-frosted sidewalk. Its flat, pristine surface contrasted with the bare, rough earth on either side of it. He disappeared from sight around a curve, toward the double doors beyond the front steps she'd seen when they pulled in.

A light came on in the house almost immediately. As big as the house was, she supposed people could be in rooms at the back of it and no one would know since there weren't lights on in the front.

So much for assuming no one lived here, Lori thought with a sinking feeling. She didn't want to meet anyone. She didn't want to visit someone in a cold castle. She didn't want to share Kris—or Andy—with total strangers.

He'd left his car keys, she noticed irritably. She and Kris could just leave if he didn't return shortly. Ten long minutes later, she was seriously considering it.

The garage door started to rise, startling her. A pair of legs—Andy's—appeared in the headlights. As soon as the door was level with his sweater-clad shoulders, he ducked under it and came to the driver's seat. He'd removed his coat. He shivered as he put the car in gear and drove into the garage.

"Andy?"

"Dinner will be served in ten minutes, madam," he said, shutting off the engine. "Be patient just a little longer." Andy leaned in to get Kris, seat, spare blanket and all. "Get Kris's bag," he instructed, taking off for the interior garage door without further ado.

Grabbing the small bag holding diapers, a couple of bottles and a change of clothes, Lori followed more slowly. She half expected someone to be waiting to greet her when she stepped inside the room off the garage. Shadows and silence welcomed her instead.

She could just see in the diffused light coming down a wide hall. Her footsteps thudded hollowly against the bare subflooring as she followed the light.

"In here," Andy called as she turned a corner into an

even wider hall. Only this wasn't a hall, she realized. It was the entry by the front doors Andy had originally come through.

The light she'd been following was a huge brass and etched-glass fixture hanging from a very long chain in the center of the two-story room. It was swathed in brown paper and plastic, probably to protect it from the paint and finish work that was still to come. Through another wide arch, Andy was spreading Kris's extra blanket before a sputtering fireplace.

"Welcome to my parlor," he said with some amusement at her expression.

"Said the spider to the fly?" She turned the phrase into a question as she hovered in the archway leading into the room.

"I am hungry," he warned with a predatory look that should have made her nervous. Instead, she felt a flutter of anticipation. "You may have something to worry about."

He'd stationed Kris's little seat close to the door. Not too far away, a dusty, paint-spattered electric heater glowed. The baby was still sleeping soundly.

"This is your house?"

"Will be as soon as it's finished," he told her, throwing another small piece of scrap lumber on the fire. It looked like it might eventually turn into a pleasant little blaze. "I usually check in at least once a week to see how the work's coming along. This is the first chance I've had this weekend."

"And the builder doesn't mind that we're here?"

Andy shrugged. "He gave me a key. He's a friend of mine," he added. "I'll call him later tonight, leave a message so his crew won't think they've had uninvited guests partying here over the holidays."

"And it's *all* just yours?" she asked, her voice rising in disbelief.

He laughed. "You sound like my mother. It is big," he admitted. "Here. Let me take your coat. It's warming up finally."

Lori bent for a closer look at Kris. "She's okay?"

"Sure. And this—"

Lori started as someone pounded at the front door.

"Looks like dinner's here." Andy modified what he'd been about to say, moving her aside in the doorway with both hands on her arms as he passed to answer the knock.

"Mr. McAllister?"

"You found us," Andy confirmed.

"You're right, man," Lori heard the delivery boy say. "Only house on the street with a light on. Didn't have a bit of trouble finding it without a number."

Andy drew a handful of cash from his jeans pocket.

"You live here?" The boy's voice held the curiosity Lori felt.

"Not yet," Andy assured him, stepping farther in to hand Lori one of the white bags. "But soon."

"Thanks," she heard the kid say when Andy told him to keep the change. The door shut quietly.

"You going stand there like a statue?" Andy asked close to her ear. His hand lightly touched the small of her back again. "Come in. Let's eat." His slight nudge moved her forward.

He settled the two bags he carried onto the corner of the blanket he'd laid over the bare floor.

"Lori?"

His low voice reanimated her. Reclaiming the sack he'd handed her, he placed it with the other two and helped her shrug out of her coat. He crossed the floor to nestle it with his own on the middle step of a ladder

standing in one corner. His hand swept in the direction
of Kris's small blanket, inviting her to sit down.

Still feeling dazed, she slumped onto the spot he indicated.

His hand hovered over the bag closest to him. "I
wanted to show you my house. I wanted to take you to
dinner. I thought we'd kill two birds with one stone."
He smiled coaxingly. "I hope you like Chinese."

"Love it," she assured him.

He grinned. "It's not the Waldorf but...added bonus.
If Kris gets fussy, we don't have to worry about her
disturbing other diners," Andy pointed out. "Let's see
what we've got." Automatically rising to her knees, Lori
helped him take a multitude of small containers from the
bags.

Outside the wall of multipaned, curtainless windows,
the black night closed in, cocooning them. The small fire
burned steadily now. Firelight flickered over Andy's
classically handsome face as he concentrated on divvy-
ing up the variety of food he'd ordered.

Lori drizzled sweet and sour sauce from a little packet
on one of her crab rangoons. "Why didn't we just stop
at a drive-through?" she asked. "Why did you have it
delivered?"

"Hot," he exclaimed around his first bite of egg roll,
blowing and panting at the same time. The word did
double duty. "I never manage to get take-out food home
this hot. For some reason, they don't seem to have the
same problem. Besides," he continued when his mouth
was no longer occupied, "I wanted time to start a fire
and warm things up and get us settled before we ate."

He'd swept some of the sawdust out of the way, she
noted. A broom stood on one side of the room, guarding
a small pile of dust and carpenter's debris. She suspected
he had better nesting instincts than she did.

"It looks almost finished," she commented, squinting toward the hall. The ceilings had been spray painted. The electrical outlets were bare, but obviously working. "When will you be able to move in?"

"Three or four weeks. All that's left is the finish work. Amazing, isn't it? A week ago, they were still putting up Sheetrock."

"What are you going to do with a house this big?" she managed to ask casually.

"Live in it," he said blithely.

By yourself? she wanted to probe. There couldn't be anyone too important in the picture, she realized. If there was, wouldn't that special person expect *some* of the attention he'd been sharing so generously with her and Kris? Why wouldn't *she* Christmas shop with him? Or come with him for his regular inspections?

Or go to a special event with him, come to think of it? Lori was certain he hadn't had a date the evening he stopped by in his tux. Was that only last night? she wondered, shaking her head. It seemed like a lifetime. Andy—and Kris—seemed like a permanent part of it.

"I have to admit, this wasn't in my plans a year ago," Andy continued, breaking into her thoughts.

"But?"

"The older neighborhood I was living in—smaller house," he said in an aside, "was being 'revitalized'. In layman's terms," he explained, "that means some developers wanted to put in a shopping mall. They offered me, and the neighbors for about four blocks around me, great prices for our houses." He shrugged. "It was a good deal, and my buddy—my builder friend—convinced me I might as well build what I wanted instead of buying something else."

"And that's why you're living at the apartment complex."

He nodded. "The developers wanted possession—they tore my house down—about three months ago. Closing on this house is scheduled for late January," he finished.

And you can afford this? she wanted to ask, looking around. Her eyes had adjusted to the dark now. Beyond the room they were in, and farther back at the far end of the stately entry, a wide, open staircase curved up into darkness.

From outside, the home looked gigantic—at least four bedrooms, she guessed, maybe even five. The large room—smaller than this room but large nevertheless—on the other side of the entry was obviously going to be a formal dining room, perfect for entertaining. The double doors she'd noted across the hall opposite it probably led to the kitchen.

This house was confirmation that he was even more out of her league than she'd imagined. Seeing him at the apartment complex had somehow put him at an accessible level. He wasn't. She didn't know her reaction to that daunting realization was vocal until he leaned forward.

"What? What's the matter, Lori?" His low voice held concern.

She hid her dismay behind a cough. "Wrong pipe," she whispered. She hoped he didn't notice she hadn't taken a bite in a while. She gave him a bright smile. "I guess I shouldn't try to eat when I'm in shock," she admitted. "Who would have guessed?"

She'd known. She'd known he was from a different world the second he walked into her apartment looking like he belonged somewhere else. In the back of her mind, she'd let herself pretend otherwise.

"Guessed what?"

"I thought..."

"What did you think, Lori?"

She shook her head in bewilderment. "I'm sorry. I thought you were a common, ordinary lawyer." His was a world she glimpsed when she entertained VIPs in her job, but one, she realized now, she only felt safe seeing from a suitable distance. "This is a…a…friggin' mansion, Andy."

Her amazement made him chuckle. "Not quite," he contradicted. "Just a big house."

"Can you really afford it?" she asked, then wished she'd kept biting her tongue.

Andy found that comment amusing, too. "That's what worries you? You're afraid I'm going to expect your fees to pay for it?" he teased.

She felt her heart lurch at the thought. "Good grief, I hope not."

He laughed and relaxed full-length on his side, half on, half off the blanket. With his head propped on one hand, he used the other to take a bite of the moo goo gai pan into his very nice mouth. He managed to get it there with chopsticks as easily as Lori used the plastic fork the Chinese restaurant had also supplied. His casual sophistication—or at least her sudden awareness of it— dazzled her. And the look he gave her between narrowed lids made her heart beat faster. "You think I'm willing to live beyond my means?"

"Of course not, but…"

He waited.

She lifted one shoulder. "Somehow, I guess I didn't think of you fitting in a house—" her hand-sweeping gesture was expansive "—a neighborhood like this."

"Why?"

She wasn't sure why. She only felt certain he was way out of her class—which she already knew. This house just hammered it home. "Maybe because I can't see myself fitting in here.'' She'd been thinking he was like her, she admitted to herself. She shrugged. "Why would you want to live somewhere like this by yourself?"

He frowned thoughtfully. "I won't be by myself forever."

"Then there is someone..."

His expressive eyes held her gaze. "Not yet," he finally said. "Why can't you see yourself fitting in here?" he asked softly.

"It's too... It seems too permanent," she modified.

His slow, electric-white smile caught her off guard. "Exactly," he said. "The house I was in was okay, but it was in a fairly upwardly mobile but transient neighborhood. A goodly number of singles. Lots of young couples. People stopping long enough to get a foothold or just passing through, transferred to the area for a year or so. I bought my house there the day I passed the bar exam. It was the right thing to do at the time and convenient, only six blocks from the office."

"But?"

"But it wasn't exactly where governors expect to find their judges."

"Their judges?"

"I'm up for a judicial appointment," he said simply, but his jaw squared. "It's where I've been headed since I first visited my father's courtroom when I was small. It's why I went to law school."

"Your father's a judge?"

"He's a lawyer." Andy half smiled. "A very good one. He used to get upset with me for being more impressed with the judges than I was with him. The minute I started considering building this house," he continued, "I started thinking it was time to throw my hat in the ring for the next opening on the bench."

"So you started building this house and immediately decided you were ready for a judicial appointment."

"I threw my hat in the ring as soon as I realized *I* was the thing holding myself back," he corrected. "I would have done that eventually, whether I decided to build this house or not. But this house does project a stable, dependable image. I hope it says I'm successful, I'm a part of this community, I'm going to be here awhile, I have responsibilities I take seriously."

"You don't like what you're doing now?"

"Yes and no." He eyed her thoughtfully. "I don't know if I can explain. My family accuses me of being on a power trip," he said with a touch of humor. "And they're right, I suppose. I want to make a difference. Judges get to play God."

"Don't you make a difference now?"

"For the most part, what I do is cut-and-dried. I find and present facts. A judge or jury rules on whether they like my interpretation of them better than they like the other guy's."

She couldn't help but grin. "You win all the time, I'll bet." How could he not? He exuded an air of everything's-going-to-be-all-right, even when he was warning her not to expect too much where Kris was concerned. That was exactly what had kept her calm since he'd entered her life.

He didn't contradict her. "But I never get a say in what happens after a decision has been made. And it drives me crazy. I want to have a say in what happens last. There are so many variables."

"What do you mean?"

"Take two guys who rob convenience stores." He hesitated. "Neither one is right, but if one of them does it because he gets a kick out of it and it's his fourth time since he was seventeen, and the other guy does it because he's desperately afraid he can't pay his baby's medical bills, there's a difference.''

"So there should be a difference in the end result.''

"Exactly. Take you and Kris," he went on to clarify. "The fact that you didn't call the authorities tells me you yourself know you don't fit the customary foster parent guidelines at all.''

"And if you were the judge in the case?''

"I'd have the flexibility to bend any rules and regulations. But I do have an advantage. I've seen you in action.''

"Oooh, that's a scary thought," Lori said, trying to keep her tone light despite how deeply his compliment touched her.

"Unfortunately, any judge we present the case to is going to be dealing with cold, hard facts.''

"You could offer to personally supervise me or whatever it's called," she suggested offhandedly.

He was shaking his head before she even finished the sentence. "You've been watching too many reruns of *Law & Order*," he teased. "It wouldn't fly.''

"Not even if you were the judge?''

"I'd have to recuse myself.''

"And that means?''

"I'd have to excuse myself from the case because I'm too personally involved. Conflict of interest.''

"You'd have to disqualify yourself *because* you know the facts.''

His jaw tightened. "Justice is supposed to be blind.''

"That seems so backward.''

"In a way," he agreed, studying her too intently. "But I can understand how personal feelings could get in the way of justice.''

Lori forked a lumpish bit of rice and concentrated on

swirling it around in the remaining sauce on her small plate. "And you're into justice?"

He nodded. "With a capital *J*."

"Well, Your Honor," she said lightly, "as much as I hope you get your appointment, I'm glad you're still an attorney. I like having 'justice' on my side."

Andy gave her a wry look. "I'll probably be an attorney for some time yet," he said ruefully. "The governor obviously wasn't as impressed with me in person as he was with me on paper."

"How could he not be impressed?"

"I didn't treat his holiday get-together with enough reverence. But it's okay. I'll get another shot."

Lori frowned. Why had he said it as if he were reassuring her? Then the shoe dropped. "Oh, Andy," Lori lamented, "that's where you were going last night?"

He glanced up sheepishly, confirming her suspicions.

"Oh, Andy. I'm sorry." She'd messed things up for him. "I didn't—"

"Hey," he interrupted, "that wasn't the only strike against me. I'm younger than the competition, for one thing. By at least ten, probably fifteen years. I knew that would be a disadvantage. Being single doesn't help, either."

Hence the desire for a stable image. Things made more sense now. And Andy had risked his dream for her and Kris. Knowing what she knew about babies now, she realized he'd risked a lot more than that. He hadn't even worried about a mess when he'd put Kris across the shoulder of his tuxedo last night.

Beneath her smile, Lori felt an almost painful surge of…gratitude. Reaching across the scattered carryout bags and cartons, she laid her fingers on his arm. "Thanks, Andy," she said. "I didn't know."

"It doesn't matter." He turned his hand and caught her fingers.

"What's wrong with the governor?" she teased. "You looked great in a tux."

She expected the smile he returned. She didn't expect the challenging admiration in his narrowed eyes. "You thought so, huh?"

She flushed. She didn't intend it to sound quite so appreciative.

"So why does all of this matter, Lori?" He gave a cursory glance at the room around them and tightened his grip on her fingers. "Why do I get the feeling that bringing you here has changed something?"

"I...I'm not sure," she lied, trying to disentangle their hands. "It just does."

His thumb slowly circled one knuckle, then another, sending nerve-racking sensations up her arm.

In the past fifteen minutes, a lot of her impressions had changed. She saw clearly that she was fascinated and a little more than infatuated with him. Without consciously thinking it, she'd been hoping for some kind of relationship with him. At the very least, a long-term friendship.

Tonight had been a wake-up call. He was way out of her reach. He didn't even live in her world. He was too permanent. Too stable. She gave up all pretense of not struggling against his hold on her.

He released her. "How does it change things?"

"All this—" she gestured behind her, around her, toward the door "—has to color the way you see things."

"You think this puts me out of touch with normal—and I use the term 'normal' loosely—people?"

"It could make a difference," she endorsed his interpretation. It beat letting him know her qualms were personal. "How could it not?"

Andy's mouth twisted in a grin. "Did you think that before I brought you here?"

Of course she'd known there was a huge chasm between them before they'd come here. She just hadn't known it mattered to her.

Thankfully, he didn't wait for an answer. "Would it surprise you to find I grew up in a house pretty much like this? Maybe even a little bigger? Definitely more stately."

"You did?"

"Like I said, my father's a successful attorney. His father before him was one, too. In fact, my grandfather served as the state's attorney general for over sixteen years. *His* father was on the Kansas Supreme Court. I've never lived any differently than this."

"So you're one of the 'privileged' class," Lori quipped nonchalantly, trying to revive their former light-hearted tone.

"Actually," Andy drawled, "if you mean I've always had everything I wanted—no. My parents are old-fashioned. They believed in making us earn our wants. I've always had everything I needed."

"Oh."

He rose from his languid sprawl. "But why do I get the feeling we're not talking about just money or houses?"

"We aren't." They were talking about an attitude toward life, expectations. She could never match his. The realization that she *wanted* to meet his expectations filled her with despair. "We're also talking about judicial appointments," she said lightly. She rose to her knees. With him towering over her that way, she couldn't think. "I want you to know that if judges were elected—like I thought they were—I'd vote for you in a minute."

"Thanks." Andy caught her hands, pulled her to her

feet, turning her toward him. Her chest was close enough to brush against him if either of them breathed deeply. "Before we get too far off the subject of houses," he said, absently pushing a short strand of hair behind her ear, "I want to talk to you about going with me to my parents' home."

"What?" Her pulse was throbbing so hard in her throat that she almost couldn't get the word out.

"I want to take you and Kris home with me tomorrow," he said. "For Christmas."

"Why?" She would have stepped away, but his hands dropped to her shoulders.

"I think you're doing a great job of taking care of Kris," Andy told her, hurrying ahead, "so don't read lack of trust into this."

He read her mind almost before she could think something. That talent awed her.

"I talked to my mother about your situation—"

"I thought the whole point was to keep this all quiet. You promised me three days. Now you've told the manager. Your mother…"

"Works for the law firm. She's one of our part-time receptionists."

The finger he placed on her lips stilled her for only an instant. She leaned away from it. "Who else are you going to tell, Mr. Lawyer? Are you forgetting," she prodded for good measure, "I *bought* your confidentiality?"

"I'm not forgetting a damn thing," he said with a quiet intensity. "Hear me out, okay? What I have to say makes perfect sense. You don't have to lay on the defensive sarcasm."

Anytime she felt the slightest bit threatened, she resorted to sarcasm. How dare he know that. He'd figured out so much—too much—about her. For a particle of a second, she resented Kris for putting her in a position that forced herself to expose so much to him. The thought passed as quickly as it had come but left a trace of guilt behind.

He moved even closer, putting his arm around her. "When most new mothers bring babies home from the hospital," he started, "*their* mothers are with them to help with the baby, to make sure the new mother gets enough rest." His free hand lifted to her face. His thumb stroked the sensitive skin beneath her eyes.

Lori knew there were dark smudges there.

"My mom could fill that gap. And answer questions..." His words trailed off.

"You've answered every one of my questions," she said softly, laying a hand on Andy's chest as much to maintain a little distance between them as anything else. She felt his heart under the heavy sweater.

"I'm a real amateur compared to my mother." His gaze rested on her mouth for a moment.

"I hope you know I do appreciate all you are doing." She glanced over at the baby. Andy's family was going to be as experienced and confident as he was. Possessive, protective qualms surged to mix with envy. Kris would be in great hands—much better than Lori's. She did want to do what was right for Kris. She wavered.

"Trust me," Andy added as if he knew she was weakening. "I'm going to do everything I can to help you keep Kris."

"I believe with all of my heart that you'll work out everything exactly as it's supposed to be."

"Then you should know I believe with all *my* heart that taking you and Kris home with me is a step toward *making* everything turn out right," he said.

"But we can't just barge in. Won't your mother—"

"It was her idea," he said. "I was smart enough to realize it was a great one."

"Okay, Mr. Attorney," she said, caving in. She couldn't afford any more of this kind of hands-on persuasion that made it so hard to think. "I guess I should be smart enough to accept the advice I'm paying you for."

He smiled for a moment. "And that brings us to another thing," he said. "I guess I should warn you of another decision...."

"Yes?" She didn't like his tone.

"I'm not going to represent you any longer."

CHAPTER SEVEN

TRUST me! He'd said trust me. "Why?" The word was out of her mouth before she could stop it. It echoed around the empty room and the hurt in her voice reverberated back to her. She'd trusted him *too* much. She'd known she'd regret it.

She saw his concern and quickly tried to mask her dismay. "Never mind." How many times did you have to be betrayed before you realized, once and for all, that trusting someone else with your hopes was like handing them a weapon to use against you. "You don't owe me an explanation. You've already done more than—"

His finger stilled her again. "Let me finish?"

She eyed him warily.

"I'm recusing myself like I'd have to if I were a judge in this case." His grin was tentative, coaxing, as he waited for her to respond. She refused. "I've been responding to this as a unique situation that calls for a unique approach, but frankly, when I volunteered to watch Kris this morning and suggested you go shopping, I *knew* I'd gone overboard. I'm *too* involved. What happens to you and Kris has become very personal."

The way he looked at her made her a mass of nervous frustration. "I *want* someone to represent us who cares what happens to Kris." She lifted her chin. "If you're too personally involved, that's fine with me."

"You deserve the best representation you can get, Lori. You need someone who doesn't have to worry about missing the forest because he's too close to the trees."

She brushed her hands together and backed away from him. She wasn't going to beg. "Okay. I can find some-one else." Her voice was flat. "I know I haven't—"

"Lori, I'm turning the case over to my sister," he interrupted in a tight voice. "She happens to be a very good attorney," he went on. "She's also a partner in my father's law firm, so your retainer applies to her, too. Though we have a general practice, Dad does a lot of business stuff. That's his specialty. I do most of the criminal law. Melanie gravitates toward the family stuff. Divorces. Wills. She's handled lots of adoptions. I've only handled two and they were pretty routine. She may have some insight I don't."

"Oh."

"I'll be around. Watching, offering any ideas—which I still don't have—but my official capacity will be as…an interested party. A friend."

"Kris's friend?"

His smile tilted. "Yes." The hint of a dimple showed even in the dim light of the barren room. "My father will also have a say, I imagine. That's one reason we're so good."

He didn't even realize he was bragging. It was part of his charm, Lori decided grudgingly.

"We all bring a different view to each case," he con-tinued. "That's another reason I plan to take you home. Bright and early the day after Christmas, we have to know what we're going to do next. Three lawyers for the price of one. Not a bad deal, Lori."

She looked at the baby who was wiggling in her little carrier. She'd be awake soon. "Kris needs all the friends she can get right now, doesn't she?"

"She does." Andy's hand moved to Lori's back. The tempo of her heart increased again. With a satisfied grin, he pulled her close in a protective gesture. All the space in the world wouldn't have allowed her to breathe. He lifted her face to his with one finger beneath her chin. "Quit fighting me, Lori," he said gently. "We're in this together. Don't sell me so short. Let me do the best I can for you. Okay?"

"Okay."

"And Lori…" His gaze held steady until she met his eyes. "Don't sell yourself short, either." He paused. "You deserve good things. There's nothing wrong with expecting them."

Suddenly, right now, what she expected and wanted more than anything was a kiss. The thought came from nowhere…and stayed until Andy gently put her away from him. She was glad the light was dim so he couldn't see her flush. She hoped he didn't read her mind now.

"Now," he said, "wanna take a quick look at my house before she—" his head dipped in Kris's direction "—wakes up?"

"Will we be able to see it in the dark?"

"A few of the light fixtures are up." He pointed to the hall. "And I stashed a flashlight here months ago."

It was the most harmless suggestion he'd made in ages. "I'd love to see it."

"Good." He held out his hand. "I'd love to show it off."

By the time Andy finished showing her the house—and he thought she was suitably impressed—Kris was wide awake and squalling for her dinner.

Andy took them back to Lori's apartment and suggested he keep Kris company while Lori packed and did whatever she needed to do so they could leave for his parents' house around ten the next morning.

Lori grabbed at his offer. He heard her moving around

the bedroom while he prowled the living room looking
for some way to make himself useful.

He tapped on the bedroom door a few minutes later.
"Is there anything I can help you with?"

"I'm about finished," she returned. "Is Kris asleep?"

Her voice was the voice of the Lori he'd caught
glimpses of from time to time today. This was the
woman who handled the world competently, who entertained and charmed VIPs for the city, the woman who
managed without "close relationships".

He decided he hated talking through a door. "No,"
he said with a shade of sarcasm, "I decided she was old
enough to fend for herself."

He heard Lori's chuckle and wished he could see her.
Her smiles were all too rare. "Does that say something
about *your* age? Are you approaching senility?"

He smiled back...through the door. "She's asleep,"
he assured her.

Now that he'd told Lori that he was turning her case
over to Melanie, was he free to do exactly what he
wanted? He planned to make it one of his personal ob-
jectives to make her smile more often.

"How old are you anyway?" she asked, breaking into
his thoughts.

"Old enough to know better," he muttered.

"What?"

"Thirty-four," he answered more loudly.

"You still there?" she called after a long moment of
silence.

"Yeah."

"You can come in now," she said.

He didn't hesitate.

She was sitting in the middle of a double bed—the
very sight made him break out in a cold sweat—surrounded by bright wrapping paper and ribbons. The

night table held a stack of beautifully wrapped gifts. Larger packages spilled over the floor and halfway around the bed.

"Kris is going to unwrap all of these herself?"

Lori's eyes were as bright as the bows scattered around her. "She may need some help," she admitted, trying hard to look serious. "If you'll get the Christmas-tree box, I thought we could put these in that."

"Good idea," he agreed. He went to get the box. By the time he returned, she had most of the mess picked up and was stuffing bows and ribbon into a small sack.

"I don't want my bows to get smashed," she explained as she carefully started loading the box with packages. "I'll have a chance to put the finishing touch on these at your parents, won't I?"

He had a finishing touch he wanted to put on something himself. Her mouth looked too somber.

"Lots of time," he told her, thinking of the initiation she was going to get into the world of parenthood at Christmastime. "Tomorrow night about this time, Jeff and Allison will be putting together a bike for their old-est son, Kevin. And Mom and Melanie will have every-one blowing yellow balloons at two o'clock in the morn-ing."

She paused to look up at him. "Yellow balloons?"

She was too prim to be talking about yellow balloons. "She has this thing for them." Far too prim. "It's a family tradition. You'll hear the whole story," he prom-ised. They were on their hands and knees as he handed her the package farthest from her.

She looked too inviting. Kissing her seemed to be all he could think about now. He was too tired of resisting. He leaned over and planted a quick kiss right on her lips. Though he'd never tasted anything quite so sweet, somehow he managed to pull himself away.

Parted in surprise, her mouth looked dew fresh from his brief taste. She'd frozen in place. Her eyes were closed.

"Hey." He reached out and touched her cheek.

Her eyelids slowly rose, launching another degree in his temperature as she revealed her overbright emerald eyes.

"Why?" she whispered.

"I wanted to," he answered in his most matter-of-fact voice and leaned toward her to do it again.

She was too quick for him. She jumped up and retreated to the far side of the room. He watched her staccato movements as she grabbed a suitcase from the back of the closet.

"I...you..." She broke off to study one of the latches on a small case she was about to pack. She carefully avoided looking at him.

"Would you mind taking that stuff to the living room while I pack a few things?" She swept from the room without waiting for an answer.

"Lori?"

"Yes?" She paused outside the door, still studiously refusing to look his way.

"I'm..." He meant to apologize but he couldn't. He wasn't sorry about a thing. "I didn't mean to offend you."

She glanced his way but her gaze lifted only to his chin. "You didn't offend me," she said softly, wincing even as she said it. "I wish you had."

"I don't understand."

"I liked it. Too much," she added, looking down at her hands clasped side by side on the suitcase handle. "I...you..." She finally looked him directly in the eyes.

For a pulse-stopping moment, he thought he saw a tear shimmer there. He rose.

She held up a hand, stopping him as he took a step toward her. "Please, Andy."

He hesitated.

She managed a grimace he thought was intended to be a grin. "Please, it's just not right."

"My resignation is official, Lori. I called Melanie as soon as we got back here. She agreed to take your case."

"I...that's not it, Andy. It's me," she said quietly. "And I just don't think you should do that again."

Lifting her head, she hurried away.

As soon as he finished lugging her box of presents to the other room, Lori sent him to his own apartment. She needed to sleep while Kris was and he had to pack his things if they were going to leave in the morning. He'd gone reluctantly.

Lori clasped the last fastener on the soft-sided nylon bag she'd packed and sank weakly beside it on her bed. She didn't think her legs would hold her any longer.

It was her worst nightmare come true. Mr. Andrew McAllister was the man she'd always been afraid she'd meet. Solid. Smart. Stable. Dependable. The kind of man who would give a lot without thought but who'd expect—and deserved—a lot in return.

Deep in her heart, she'd suspected it. She'd forced herself not to think of him that way. She'd willed herself to suspect every little thing—like bringing the apartment manager and saying he wasn't going to represent her anymore—as betrayals.

Thinking that way kept her from thinking of Andy in other ways. She'd even convinced herself his involvement—his conflict of interest or whatever—was only Kris. It was obvious the man had a soft spot for babies. And this particular one was defenseless, sweet. She could capture anyone's heart just by waving that tiny little baby hand.

But it was Lori's heart that had gone haywire when he'd touched her or pulled her close. She'd told herself he acted in the same comforting way with all his clients. She'd reacted to his concern, the gentle caresses, just like all his clients did. It was all part of his legal bag of tricks.

She'd managed to make herself believe her feelings were a case of extreme gratitude or appreciation. She hadn't let herself *think* this way for more than a minute.

And then he'd kissed her.

One harmless kiss. But it had changed everything. She let one of the tears she'd been holding back spill down her cheek and waver unattended at the edge of her mouth.

The mouth Andy had kissed.

The tear tasted salty as she caught it on her tongue. Damn him. Why had he done it?

The tension and lack of sleep for the past couple of days were beginning to take their toll and she felt a bone-deep weariness. She was too tired to pretend any longer that his interest was all in the baby. She couldn't pretend the heightened emotions she had been buffeted by were all because of Kris.

She was attracted to him like no other man had ever attracted her. It would take all of two seconds to fall in love with him—if she let herself.

She couldn't let herself.

What made it worse, much more difficult, was that he was attracted to her, too. It would be so easy just to let herself fall. "Disaster," she muttered. "It would be a disaster."

She didn't know if it was possible to have a broken heart but something in her chest hurt like hell. She didn't

want to feel it. But she couldn't let whatever was blooming and growing inside her blossom any further. She had
to nip it in the bud, pull it out by the roots. Life had
never seemed so unfair.

"Oh, God, please let me have Kris," she whispered,
disregarding the tears that insisted on coming. "Don't
make me give up both of them. Please."

She glanced at her watch. She had to get some sleep.
If she wasn't careful, she'd wake up in the morning with
puffy eyes. Shoot, Andy would see them; he'd probably
say exactly the right thing and make her want to love
him all the more.

She hurried to the bathroom to slap cold water on her
face. She stiffened her spine. She'd had practice at this.
She could handle it.

Tomorrow, she and Kris would be with Andy's family. Thank goodness, there'd be too many distractions
for her to fall in love.

Kris had had her breakfast and bath and Lori had finished packing Kris's things by the time Andy rang the
doorbell the next morning.

He searched Lori's face a little too closely as she let
him in. "Kris kept you up all night again?"

She managed to smile impersonally. Babies were nice
in ways Lori had never imagined, great excuses for all
sorts of things. She let him think what he wanted. "I'll
be fine."

"You should have let me stay."

She couldn't even respond to that. "Are we ready?"
she asked as brightly as she could manage.

"We just have to load your things in the car."

"That's it." She pointed to the area beside the hall
closet. The small bag she'd packed for herself sat beside

the large bag she'd put Kris's things in. "The box with the presents should probably go first. It's the biggest."

"And the box in the kitchen," he reminded her. He'd put formula and diapers and baby paraphernalia in it last night.

"Oh, yes."

"I'll take these down while you bundle Kris up in the new snowsuit. Then you can bring her and I'll get the suitcases. We'll be on our way."

"Listen," she heard herself say, "I've been thinking. Maybe I should take my car, just in case—"

"You think you might need to make a quick get-away?"

She briefly meet his gaze. "You never know."

She thought she'd stayed far enough away from him. She was wrong. Even though he wasn't touching her, even through his heavy coat, she could feel his warmth. She could feel him breathe in and out beside her.

He studied her. "You won't have any reason to run."

She backed away a step and felt him resist the urge to follow. "That's not what—"

His eyebrows arched disbelievingly.

She hadn't lied to him yet. She had to be honest with him now. "Okay," she agreed. "That *is* what I was worried about. But don't you think it would be a good idea to have options? Things *can* happen."

"After everyone gets there, there will be a minimum of five cars at Mom and Dad's house," he said dryly. "I—or someone—will take you anywhere you want to go, Lori. All you have to do is tell us where and when." When she still hesitated, he added, "You haven't driven with a baby in your car. You sure you want to?"

Come to think of it, it might be more of a distraction than she was ready to handle. Kris's safety *did* have to be her first concern. "You're right. Okay."

Since it was a gloomy day, Lori hadn't opened the blinds or drapes so she didn't have those to close. A cursory check through the apartment and within minutes they were ready to go.

Andy stood by the door with Kris while Lori turned out the lights and grabbed her purse. Lori joined him and flipped the last switch. She'd forgotten the Christmas tree in the corner. "I shouldn't have wasted my money," she murmured more to herself than to him.

He caught her arm. "It wasn't a waste, Lori. Whatever else I said, a Christmas tree is not a waste of money."

"No?" She smiled up at him.

"Definitely not."

"Then you won't mind if we take it with us?" she asked lightly.

That left him speechless.

"I'm kidding," she offered, wondering if the easy camaraderie they'd shared before the kiss could ever be recaptured. "It's a good thing I got a fake one. I can always put it back in the box for next...for sometime. Right?"

"Right."

She walked across the room and pulled the plug. In the late December morning with all the curtains drawn, the room was cast in instant darkness. She slowly made her way to the man and baby silhouetted in the light from the hall by the door before she looked back.

Where fairy lights and brightly colored bulbs had shone only seconds ago, there seemed to be a shadowy, triangular black hole. She looked up at the man beside her and shivered with the acceptance that the space he was filling in her life would be exactly the same when this was all over. When he was gone.

Lori had handled family Christmases before. During college, she'd gone home with friends each year...until her last one. That year, they'd been so busy planning their ski trip, no one thought to ask what she was doing for the ''real'' holiday. By the time someone did, she'd pretended to have plans.

That was the year she'd discovered that Christmas was easier to take if she just climbed into a hole and pulled it in around her, waiting for the holiday to be over. There was no pressure to perform, no pressure to act overjoyed when she received an impersonal fruit basket or bubble-bath set for Christmas. She didn't have to find gifts for people she hardly knew.

She bit her lip. Should she have gotten Andy's parents something? She hadn't even thought about it. Who all would be at their house? Her stomach tightened with the all-too-familiar panic.

No one would expect it, she decided quickly. For one thing, no one but Andy's mom and dad knew they were coming. Since it was Christmas Eve, by the time the rest of his family discovered an intruder in their midst, no one would have a chance to worry about a present for her. A sure way to make them all feel guilty would be to get something for each of them.

Maybe a hostess gift? A selection of jams and jellies or something for his mom they could all share?

Grabbing Andy's arm, she pointed to the mall just ahead. ''Can we stop? I thought of something I need.''

Andy flipped on his turn signal.

''I'll only be a few minutes,'' she promised and he looked amused.

''I had to stop here anyway,'' he said. ''I have to pick up the presents I forgot to get last night.''

''Oh, yeah,'' Lori said, shaking her head. She'd forgotten all about them. Just like she'd almost forgotten to cancel her ski trip. She'd had to stop and do it right before they'd left her apartment this morning. Such a small price to pay if she was able to keep Kris. "Shall I meet you there, at the wrapping booth?" she asked as she unfastened her seat belt. "I'll get mine wrapped, too."

"Sounds good."

She hesitated, her hand hovering on the door handle. "Do you mind watching Kris for a moment?"

He gave her a wry look.

He'd been helping her take care of the baby for two days now without a murmur of complaint. "I guess you haven't minded yet, have you? But I thought...well, your presents will take both hands to carry."

"Start acting as if I'm doing you a favor," he warned only half-jokingly, "and I may start expecting favors of my own." He licked his lip with the tip of his tongue.

It was his first reference to the kiss. The first hint that he'd even thought about it since she'd told him not to do it again. He was letting her know that anything he did now, he was doing for Kris. Lori had used up her share of goodwill.

"Good," she whispered to herself as his warning sent her scurrying to the mall.

She'd definitely have to tell him why he couldn't be interested in her, she thought. During the long, restless night, she'd even figured out how she could bring it up. Casually.

She'd admitted she liked his kiss after all. It was only fair. She had to be straightforward and honest with him. When she told him why they couldn't get involved, he would understand....

By the time she brought her selection of imported jams and jellies and syrups to the little booth, he was waiting there with Kris.

After the women in the booth finished her present, he

handed her the baby and put it with the two huge sacks of gifts sitting at his feet.

Before too much longer, they were back at the car. She fastened Kris into her seat while he filled the rest of the back seat with his presents.

"We make a good team," he said as if thinking out loud.

"It's a shame you decided to quit on me," she said dryly as they got back in the car.

He gave her a thoughtful look.

She tried to smile nonchalantly. "As my attorney," she explained, then realized he knew exactly what she meant. "Bad joke. I'm sorry."

He turned, the car keys in his hand instead of the ignition. He draped one long arm across the back of the seat. "By my count, the score's all tied up. We aren't going to start taking potshots at each other now, are we?"

She held up a hand. "I'm sorry," she repeated.

His eyes narrowed. "Does that have something to do with your reaction last night?"

"What do you mean?"

"Did you think I'd change my mind about representing you if you pretend…that there isn't anything happening between us? That you aren't interested in me?"

Oh, it was tempting. What a wonderful explanation, an easy out. And if she managed to convince him she really wasn't interested, everything could be back exactly like it was.

"Is that why you don't—"

Her heavy coat made the movement awkward, but she stopped him with mittened fingers against his mouth. Though it was his gesture, it felt right.

His eyes searched hers as she lowered her hand. She wanted to strip off the mittens and feel his warmth beneath cheeks that were ruddy from the cold. She watched the vapor from his breath.

"Your representing me has nothing to do with my not wanting you to kiss me, Andy," she said softly. She chewed on her lip and stared at the bright red car parked next to his in the busy parking lot. "You deserve the very best life has to offer." She glanced down at the hands she'd clenched together in her lap. "I can't think of a single reason why I should stop you from getting it."

His hand found her shoulder. The other tipped her chin up until she had to meet his eyes. "What the hell does that mean?" How could deep dark chocolate glint with bitter cold?

"I could fall in love with you, Andy," she said. "I don't want to. I don't want to get hurt."

"Would you give me some credit, lady? Would you quit expecting so little? What makes you think I couldn't fall in love as easily as you?"

"Maybe you could, but you shouldn't," she said thickly. She refused to let tears fill her eyes. They clogged her throat instead.

"Shouldn't that be my choice? My decision?"

"Only if you have all the facts."

"Okay," he agreed. "What ones am I missing?"

"You've said you wanted a family, Andy. You plan to have kids someday."

He nodded as his scowl grew deeper.

She wanted to smooth the lines between his brow. "I can't have children, Andy. You'd better find someone who can fill all those bedrooms in that huge house you're building." She turned and stared out the windshield. "It doesn't make any sense to let myself fall in love with you—or you fall in love with me—when I can't give you something that's so important."

opened the door, took hold of Lori's arm and
pulled her to her feet.

"Are you all right?" she whispered, then glanced
at Andy. "Is something wrong?" she said, her gaze
darting from one to the other.

CHAPTER EIGHT

ANDY'S reaction was...none. His face gradually turned
to stone. After a moment, he slipped his key in the ignition and said, "Let's go home."

The twenty-minute trip passed in silence. That hadn't
been the way she wanted to tell him. But it had worked
out, hadn't it? The information was there. He knew the
facts. He'd accepted it.

Somehow, during the long night, she'd convinced herself Andy's reaction to her news wouldn't matter, that
she wanted him to accept it without comment or emotion. She didn't realize she'd harbored a glimmer of hope
that he would say it didn't matter until she felt hope die.
Something in Lori's chest felt so tight she wished it
would soon splinter. She could hardly wait. She wanted
the painful part to be over.

Now, she had to brace herself to meet his family.

Veronica McAllister stepped out the back door as
soon as they turned into the driveway of his parents'
home. On the surface, she was exactly what Lori expected. Tall and elegant, she looked like someone chosen to be high society's Matron of the Year. Her expertly
styled dark brown hair didn't have so much as a particle
of gray in it. She shivered, wrapping her arms around
the tasteful, champagne-colored sweater. The action covered up the white snowflakes cascading down the front
and showed off her expensive manicure. She met them
almost before Andy brought the car to a stop.

Before Lori could protest, Veronica McAllister

opened the door, took little Kris out of Lori's arms and hurried into the house.

With her empty arms still outstretched, Lori glanced at Andy. He forced a grin. "Go on in," he told her. "Introduce yourself and rescue Kris. I'll unload the car."

Lori hesitantly followed the path Mrs. McAllister had taken. As she reached the door, it flew open, startling her.

"Come in. Hurry. It's cold out there," Mrs. McAllister ordered.

The door snapped closed and Lori was bustled into a brightly lit country kitchen. When she stopped in the middle of the room, Mrs. McAllister passed her and took Kris to a windowed alcove. Cooing all the while, she laid Kris down on the square oak tabletop and began to unwrap her.

"Oooh." She gently touched Kris's face and examined her tiny hands, then picked her up again. "She is precious." Mrs. McAllister glanced up. Her tear-glazed eyes annihilated Lori's preconceived notions about the woman inside the proper holiday hostess attire. "Who could desert this tiny thing?"

"I wish I knew," Lori murmured.

Veronica McAllister left the bundle of blankets and snowsuit on the table and crossed to Lori. "Andrew said you have very little experience with babies." Mrs. McAllister's soft voice held concern.

"None," she admitted. "He promised I'd learn a lot here."

Holding Kris close to her breast, Mrs. McAllister wrapped her free arm around Lori's shoulder. "You're very brave to take on something like this. I'll help anyway I can."

Lori hated empty displays of affection from strangers.

This one didn't feel empty. It was almost worse. It made the tight ache inside grow even tighter. She willed herself not to squirm or move away.

Mrs. McAllister studied Lori as she'd studied Kris. But where Kris's inspection had been filled with the kind of unconditional approval people seemed to reserve for babies, Lori's examination was analytical, intense. She shifted nervously.

Mrs. McAllister smiled. "Here. I'm being very rude. Let me take your coat." She waved an arm vaguely. "Well, I seem to have my hands full. Why don't you put your coat out there?" She indicated the small enclosed porch she'd practically pushed Lori through as they came in. "There's a coat rack.

"Can I get you some coffee?" Mrs. McAllister called out as Lori followed her directions. "Or I have hot spiced cider if you'd prefer."

"Coffee's fine, Mrs. McAllister," Lori accepted as she returned to the kitchen. The air was heavy with mouthwatering Christmassy fragrances.

"Here." Mrs. McAllister passed Kris back to her. Lori had the gratifying—maybe wrong—impression that giving Kris back was a sign that the woman had decided she was worth trusting with the child. "Call me Veronica," her hostess invited over her shoulder as she took a tall, holly-decorated mug from the cabinet over the coffeemaker.

They did the sugar-cream-or-black routine as Veronica shepherded Lori to a chair, then dipped some spiced cider from an electric crock pot sitting amid Christmas greenery.

Kris, still sound asleep, her arms flopped out like a rag doll's, snored quietly.

Veronica frowned toward the back door as she took a seat beside Lori. "Andrew should be in by now."

"Speak of the devil." Andy's voice preceded him through a wide door at the opposite end of the kitchen. "I thought I might as well put the presents under the tree," he explained. His smile for his mother seemed strained. Lori thought his usual easy grace looked stilted. "I took them in through the garage. I'll get the diapers and suitcases in a minute." He leaned down and brushed a kiss on Veronica's cheek. "You want me to put Kris and Lori's things in the den?"

Veronica sipped at her mug and murmured an "mmm". "The den's the traditional 'new' baby room," Veronica explained. "Close enough to the action that you don't miss out on anything but far enough away during the night that everyone else can sleep if she decides to have an all-nighter."

"She did better last night. Almost slept the night through. I'm hoping she'll do even better tonight."

Andy's brows rose and Lori remembered she'd let him think Kris was responsible for the dark circles under her eyes this morning. She squirmed under his scrutiny.

"Well, you're here now. If she doesn't sleep, there'll be plenty of people ready, willing and able to walk the floor with her," Veronica said. "It's almost fun when you know the sleep disruption is only temporary. There are definite advantages to being a grandmother." She showed a dimple that matched Andy's. "Here, Andrew. I'll get you some coffee. Or would you rather have some of this?" She indicated her cup.

"Not right now, thanks. Let me get the rest of the things," he declined, starting for the back door. Lori suspected he didn't want to be in the same room with her. "Where's Dad?"

"At the office." Veronica scowled and shook her head hopelessly. "He talked to Melanie after you called. They discussed a couple of options and he wanted to look something up. I suspect he also had a little Christmas shopping to do. He always waits till the last minute," she said in an aside to Lori, "but he should be home anytime."

Andy straightened. "I'll go get the bags."

As soon as he'd finished, he announced an errand he needed to run and left. Lori was almost relieved. Maybe she was imagining it, but he'd barely looked at her since she'd told him. Which was good, she reassured herself. Hadn't that been the whole point? Stunt the growth of whatever it was that made them seem so in tune?

Veronica led Lori to a cozy den, showing her the deep drawer she'd lined with a soft pillow for Kris. "And this," Veronica said as soon as they'd settled Kris in her new "bed", "pulls out into a bed for you." Removing the cushions, she demonstrated. The mattress was already made up with sheets and Veronica declined Lori's offer of help as she spread a heavy quilt over the top. "That's the bathroom," she said, waving toward a door at the end of the room.

Lori went to peek in. "It's very nice," she complimented. "I hope you know how grateful I am for…for everything."

"When Andrew helped me yesterday, I got the impression that inviting you and baby Kris might be the only way we'd get him here," she said dryly, "but don't think that's the only reason I suggested you come, Lori. I'm glad you're here for your own sake. And it's so nice to have a baby in the house for Christmas."

Kris stirred and Veronica sat down, leaning over to stroke the downy dark hair with one elegant finger. Lori joined her, sitting down on the edge of the bed.

"I don't know what I would have done without your son," she said. "By the time he came to my rescue the other night, I was a basket case. I...I've never felt so scared in my life."

"Don't worry." Veronica patted her knee. "Andrew and Melanie will find a way for you to keep her."

"It doesn't matter."

Veronica looked taken aback.

"I want to keep her more than you can imagine," Lori explained, "but only if that's what's best for her. I'm not sure my judgment isn't faulty about that."

Her hostess smiled. "Andrew's a very good judge of character. He told me no one could be better for her. That's enough for me."

"Thank you," Lori mouthed, too touched by the dual compliment to speak.

Veronica patted Lori's shoulder.

The family's predilection for touching was more than Lori could take. She used the box of Kris's things as an excuse to move away. Searching it as if she really wanted something, she found a lightweight blanket she'd brought. The corner of Kris's rosebud mouth lifted as Lori spread it carefully over her.

Touching Kris one more time, Veronica eased off the bed. "She's going to be out for a while." She rested her hand at the small of Lori's back to head her toward the door. "Come on. I need to start lunch. You can help if you'd like or you can just keep me company."

With one last peek at Kris, Lori followed Veronica from the room.

The kitchen seemed to magically fill the moment they entered it. Andy's father returned. As soon as Veronica finished the introductions, he grabbed a spoon and declared himself the official taster of the big pot of chili Veronica had put on the stove to warm.

Andy had inherited Veronica's smile. Almost everything else had clearly come from his father. John was tall, with Andy's broad shoulders, though his were a bit stooped. His thick white hair grew exactly like Andy's, including the tiny sprig that wanted to grow in a different direction from the rest at his hairline. He had the kindest blue eyes Lori had ever seen.

Veronica set Lori to peeling a sinkful of vegetables for a relish plate. She watched with quiet amusement and a large dose of envy as John and Veronica teased each other. Theirs was obviously a very durable marriage.

About the time Veronica declared the chili ready, Melanie arrived, explaining that she had left Greg, her husband, home with their two children. She had come to meet Lori and discuss some ideas. With that brief introduction, Melanie was ready to sit at the table with a cup of coffee and get down to business.

Veronica immediately called Greg to demand that he and her grandchildren "get over here".

"Mom, we're coming this evening," Melanie protested.

"So go home after lunch," Veronica said. "But there's no reason why your family should have to fend for themselves when I've made plenty. They shouldn't miss all the excitement just because you're going to work on a holiday."

The way she said the word "work" made Lori suspect the issue was a sometimes sensitive one between Veronica and the rest of her family.

"It is a holiday," Lori protested, doubting for the millionth time whether she should have let Andy talk her into this. "Surely we can wait—"

"If you don't get some of this out of the way, we'll end up talking business tonight and all day tomorrow, right through Christmas," Veronica interrupted as she got up to stir the pot on the stove. "I guess I should be grateful we have time now." She slapped at John's hand as he followed her and got yet another clean spoon from a drawer. "Cut that out," she ordered as he hovered above the chili.

"We just need to outline some kind of strategy," Melanie said.

"It smells great in here." With a pleased look on his face, Andy bustled in from the errand he'd said he had to run.

He almost looked back to normal, Lori thought, relief mixing with a tinge of sadness.

"Melanie. Why am I not surprised to find you here?" He pecked his sister's cheek. "I'm starving."

He found Lori. Something about his smile turned plastic, then softened. It said everything was all right, almost like the way it had been during the past day or two. Before the kiss.

Lori, who'd been trying to blend with the woodwork, greeted him with a self-conscious small wave.

"Let me get rid of this coat," he told the room in general, but his gaze remained on her.

By the time he returned, Melanie and John had settled on one side of the table, Veronica was pouring them all drinks again and everyone looked at Lori expectantly.

Andy took the seat beside her and draped his arm casually over the back of her chair. "So what have you come up with, Mel?"

"Dad was looking up a couple of archaic laws for me, and I haven't had a chance to check them out, but I think our best course of action will be to request an emergency hearing before Judge Everett Benson—family court—" she explained in an aside to Lori, "and buy some time. He's almost maniacally dedicated to children's welfare issues and doesn't give two cents for SRS's rules and regulations as long as we offer a *better* suggestion that doesn't break any laws. I'd bet my socks that's our best approach.''

"What does that mean?" Lori asked, entering the conversation.

Melanie continued using a mixture of legal terms and precedents and an assortment of examples. It all sounded bureaucratic and unfeeling and complex. Andy's hand circled her shoulder, lending her warmth that stopped the chill making its way up her spine.

John and Andy picked up the explanation from time to time.

"So what do I need to do?" Lori finally asked.

"We. What do we need to do," Melanie corrected. "First, let's consider your assets." Melanie picked up the pen from the center of the notepad she'd set on the table when she first arrived.

"My assets?"

"The thing any judge will look for is a stable, healthy environment for the child," John explained.

"We have to sell you to the judge," Andy said, his hand tightening momentarily. "Obviously, you've thought about it since you made a point of telling me about the job."

"That's it exactly," Melanie agreed, looking excited. "What about the job?" She poised her pen above the pad.

Lori watched her face grow more and more unrevealing as Andy explained.

"We'd best talk to your boss before we request the hearing," Melanie said. Talk to Lori's boss, she wrote on the top line of the clean pad. She underlined it three times. "That's our first step bright and early the day after Christmas."

"What exactly do you do, Lori?" John asked.

Lori got halfway through the explanation before she

saw Melanie draw a line through the only thing she'd written. "Why? Why did you do that?" From the corner of her eye, Lori saw Andy shake his head at Melanie. "Why?" she asked him.

"You're going to be requesting the court to give you custody of a newborn baby when you're single. That will be a small hurdle if we can convince the judge you're capable and caring. Unless you can quit your job, you'll have to have child care. A small strike against you, but not a major one..."

Lori's grip tightened on the edge of the table as she waited for the "but".

"...until you add in the fact that you travel...how often?"

"Probably an average of twice a month, two to three days maximum each time."

"So four or five days a month?"

Lori nodded.

"Who's going to watch Kris when you travel?" Melanie asked.

"I...I don't know. But I'll find...manage something."

"The judge is going to want to know," John said.

"So I'll have to figure it out sooner than I anticipated."

"*If* you have a job," Melanie said dryly.

"At least three of the people in my office have kids," Lori went on, ignoring Melanie's comment. "It doesn't stop them from doing what they need to do."

"Are they married?" Andy asked.

"Only two of them," Lori said defensively. She clasped her face between her hands. Melanie was telling her in gentle terms what she'd known for two days. She'd been too intent on Kris to think clearly. Wasn't wanting to take care of her more than she'd ever wanted anything worth anything?

Veronica came to her rescue. "Don't worry, hon." Her hand on Lori's back patted, rubbed, soothed. "They really aren't ganging up on you. They have to go through all this to find the right answers."

Lori glanced up at her thankfully. With one more encouraging pat, Veronica went to get the coffeepot to refill their cups.

John picked up on Andy's previous question. "Don't suppose there's a special someone around you've been hesitant to make a commitment to?" he prodded with a twinkle in his eye. "Someone you've been putting off?"

Lori felt every eye in the room on her.

Andy withdrew his arm from the back of her chair to pick up his coffee cup and take a sip. "She doesn't plan to get married," he commented.

Lori tried not to notice several raised eyebrows and smiled as brightly as she could. She hoped her face didn't crack. "Sorry."

Melanie absently wrote something else on her pad. "Long shot," she told Lori with a shrug as noises sounded at the back door.

John hurried to open it and let Melanie's family in. He came back with a dark-haired toddler in his arms. Andy rose to greet the new arrivals.

Melanie reached across and gripped Lori's hand reassuringly. "We'll continue this after lunch," she said softly. "We'll find the right combination of things to present to the judge."

Veronica came through the door at the opposite end of the room holding Kris. "Look what I found," she said.

Lori went to take the baby so Veronica could do justice to the small girl insistently saying Nana at her feet.

"I didn't even hear her," she said apologetically.

Veronica picked up her grandchild as she reassured

Lori, "There's no reason you should have. She wasn't crying. I went to check on her and she was awake. You're doing fine," she added with a comforting wink and turned her attention to her granddaughter.

Lori took Kris back to the seat she'd been occupying at the table. She sank into it and watched the chaos mount around them.

They all kissed and hugged even though Lori suspected they saw each other almost every day. The little boy, Michael, begged Andy for a piggyback ride while Melanie encouraged her angel-faced daughter to show Grandma what she'd just learned.

Andy swung Michael up on his shoulders, then pitched forward, catching him as the child swung down again. Michael laughed delightedly. Andy laughed with him. He would definitely make his lucky children a wonderful dad.

In her whole life, Lori had never felt so like a spectator on the outside looking in. She gazed down at the precious bundle in her arms and realized Kris had gripped her finger in one sweet little hand. Bringing the tiny fingers to her lips, Lori gave them a kiss and promised herself Kris would never, never feel the intense longing that threatened to debilitate her if she continued to watch the proceedings going on around them.

"This won't happen to you," she promised in a whisper, then took Kris and her freshly warmed bottle back to the den where they didn't have to see.

The rest of the day passed in a blur. Greg, Melanie's husband, put their kids down for a nap when the "legal eagles," as Veronica called them, started back at it as soon as the dishes were cleared from the table.

Only this time, Lori didn't contribute much. She listened as they discussed various cases and precedents

John had found in the heavy tomes he'd brought home from the office. Andy regularly got other books from the collection John kept at home.

Veronica shooed them at last to start dinner.

They'd barely sat down at the table when Andy's other sister, Allison, and her brood arrived from Texas.

Allison and Jeff had three children, all boys. The oldest was six, the youngest almost two. The middle one looked enough like Andy to make it difficult for Lori to breathe.

All five grandchildren obviously thought their uncle was their own special toy. They looked like stair steps as they gathered around and begged him for piggyback rides and to "swing me".

He occupied them as Greg and Jeff unloaded the car and the women expanded and reset the table. John stood on one side of the room adopting the role of traffic director as Lori stood on the other with Kris, watching again.

Andy caught her eye and winked. "Keeps me from having to go out in the cold," he mouthed as he tossed the three-year-old—the one that looked like him—gently into the air.

"Why don't you do something useful and take them all in to get washed up for dinner?" Veronica suggested dryly as she passed him to get more ice.

Allison was also an attorney, so the discussion centered around Lori and Kris's problem once they all sat down to a meal again. Lori—and Veronica, she suspected—was grateful when, after it was over, everyone's concentration turned to Christmas.

Sometime during the day, Veronica had put on Christmas music. It had been playing softly, unobtrusively in the background until someone turned it up. A huge assortment of homemade candy, cookies, gingerbread soldiers and cinnamon-glazed popcorn appeared at various places around the house.

The parents of the small children began filing them off for baths and John suggested Lori take Kris, who had become fussy, to the family room. He settled her into a high-backed, upholstered rocker, then left the two of them alone.

Lori let the muted background noise wash around her. A lamp on the end table at her side was the only light in the room besides the tree. On its branches, hundreds of multicolored fairy lights blinked in imperfect rhythm. The sharp pine scent seemed a perfect contrast to Kris's pleasant baby smell.

"You hiding?" Andy asked from behind her, startling her. He searched her face as he lowered himself to the footstool in front of her, his gaze now level with hers. "You aren't sorry you came?"

"How could I be sorry I came?" she returned, pulling Kris closer as she tried to find something else to look at besides him. "This is a beautiful house. Your mother has been wonderful. I see why a family is…so important at a time like this."

"I was afraid you might be feeling overwhelmed."

"I am." *He* overwhelmed her. His dark hair tousled from his overly energetic play with his niece and nephews. His far too analytical gaze. The beautifully white teeth that electrified his smile.

"Lori…" he started.

Michael, Melanie's pajama-clad oldest, rushed in and lunged at Andy, tackling and almost bowling him over. "Tell me what you got me, Uncle Andrew. Tell me what you got me for Christmas," he demanded. Andy grabbed the floor to maintain his balance, then turned on the child, tickling him until he was a giggling, wiggling mass of little boy.

"What makes you think I got you anything?" Andy teased.

Right behind Michael came another, then another. Andy was buried beneath kids again. Lori watched their shiny clean faces as they clung with awe to every nonsensical, ridiculous word he said.

Their eyes sparkled, Christmas anticipation mixed with their devotion to him, their much-loved uncle. She'd done the right thing, warning him off. But the lump in her throat didn't ease. He needed children of his own. A son.

One by one, John and the rest of the adults filed in. Veronica turned down the music and John sat down to read a giant, worn version of *The Night Before Christmas*. His deep, rich voice settled into a pleasant cadence that lulled Kris and at least two other grandkids to sleep. The grown-ups were as enthralled by the ritual, Lori noted, as their children, straining to see the pictures when John turned the book to his audience for that purpose.

Lori couldn't keep her eyes from Andy.

She slipped away as soon as she could after the story was over. Andy knocked at the door of the den a minute later and then came in as Lori settled Kris into her drawer.

"You calling it a night?" he asked.

She sighed. "I think I should," she whispered.

"You're going to miss the excitement. The Christmas Eve rituals *after* the kids have gone to bed," he explained as she moved to stand beside him at the door. "Putting bikes and things together. It's part of the learning experience."

"To tell you the truth," she forced herself to speak normally, the same way everyone else did around sleeping kids in this household, "I don't think my bike-putting-together-skills will be missed. And I've about had it. I'd better get some rest while she's asleep.''

"We'll try to hold it down." He touched the soft skin beneath one of her eyes with his thumb. "Let me know if you need anything."

"Thanks. I will." She wondered what he'd say if she said she needed him to hold her. Just one more time.

His gaze fell to her mouth. "You can't fool me," he accused. "You just don't want to blow up balloons." With a smile and a lazy wink that seemed to promise something good, he quietly closed the door.

CHAPTER NINE

LORI lay in bed forever, awake, listening to the muted laughter and strange noises. Despite the weariness holding her body immobile, her mind raced.

The house was finally quiet and she was almost asleep when Kris awoke and began crying.

"Oh, sweetheart," Lori moaned and dragged herself to the drawer made into a bed.

After changing Kris's diaper, Lori threw her robe on, slipped her feet into warm slippers and went to get a bottle. She almost dropped the baby as she stepped into the dimly lit kitchen—as promised, Veronica had left a light on over the sink—to find Andy standing in front of the microwave, heating Kris's 2:00 a.m. snack.

He was barefoot, bare chested. His only visible item of clothing, a faded pair of jeans, hung loosely on his hips.

"I heard her crying," he explained before Lori could ask. "Thought you might like some company."

"Thank you," she said. "Did she wake anyone else?"

"Mom."

Lori started toward one of the chairs by the table. Andy was there before her, pulling it out, turning it to face the room.

"I told her to go back to bed." He stood aside as Lori sat down. She smiled her thanks and then to avoid the look in his eyes immediately dropped her gaze. That was a mistake. His lightly tanned chest with its sprinkling of dark hair invited her examination.

Lori didn't know where to look. She expelled a long—hopefully inaudible—sigh when he went to check the bottle.

"I told Mom she could have the next stint." He grinned. "By the time Kris finishes that feeding, the kids will be up yelling that Santa's been here. I don't imagine either of you will get back to bed. It's ready," he announced, shaking some of the warm formula on the inside of his wrist the way he'd shown her. Instead of giving her the bottle, he extended his empty hand. "Come on. We'll go in the family room. You'll be more comfortable there." His fingers laced with hers as he led her down the dark hall and through the foyer.

He flipped a light switch and waded into a sea of bright yellow balloons, which littered the floor.

Pointing Lori toward the rocker, Andy handed her the bottle, then carefully picked a path to the other end of the room to plug in the Christmas tree lights. "This will be enough light and a whole lot less glare," he said.

The tree came instantly alive, casting sparks of color on the brightly wrapped presents of all shapes and sizes piled haphazardly to the center of the large room. Lori caught her breath at the sight. This was the holiday depicted on Christmas cards and TV shows.

A small bicycle, complete with training wheels, stood at one side of the tree. A child-size pink-and-purple playhouse had been erected in the corner. Stockings brimming with goodies marched the length of the mantel. One of them, Lori realized with a start, bore her name. Another held Kris's, scrawled in the same glittery green paint as hers.

"No wonder you thought my tree looked sick," she managed as he turned off the overhead light. Emotion caught at the edge of her voice. She cleared her throat.

"Did I say that?"

"Not in so many words," she admitted with a grin. "It was the way you looked at it."

Andy chuckled. "Mom's had years and years to accumulate all of this," he said. "Give yourself time."

"I'm not just talking about the tree. It's the whole thing. I always dreamed of waking up to something like this on Christmas morning. The presents. Family." This time, Lori couldn't keep the wistfulness from her tone. "Your father reading *The Night Before Christmas*." When she was small, she'd often wondered if a Christmas like the ones she'd seen on TV really existed or if it was all a fairy tale. This household proved it did. "But I don't understand the balloons. Is that some holiday thing I totally missed?"

Andy laughed again. Pleasant memories sparked from his eyes. "It's the McAllisters' very own private sign that Santa's been here." Andy had settled on the footstool in front of them. "You should have stayed up with us. You would have got to see him arrive." He pointedly stared at the mistletoe over the door. "Maybe even got to kiss him."

The image that popped into Lori's mind had nothing to do with a man with a white beard and a red suit. She *should* have stayed up. She hadn't slept anyway. Even as she thought it, Lori knew sleep wasn't why she'd gone to bed. She hadn't really wanted to know what she'd been missing all her life. "What did I miss?"

"Lots of bad language during the major construction." Andy indicated the playhouse and the bike. "Grown-up eggnog. Last-minute wrapping. And, of course, blowing up balloons."

"Oh. I didn't put the bows on my packages yet," Lori remembered out loud.

"Here." Andy immediately rose. "Let me give Kris her bottle. You can do it now." Her hand brushed his chest as she handed Kris over. Lori held her breath. She started breathing again, short, shallow gasps, when he settled in the rocking chair with Kris.

He pointed out the stack of presents he had set almost behind the tree. Lori went to find her bows and ribbon in the den where he'd stashed them.

"You still didn't tell me how this balloon thing got started," she said as she returned and cleared a space to sit on the floor beside her presents.

"Melanie started it," Andy said. "She was three and a yellow balloon was the only thing she would say she wanted for Christmas. Allison and I were performing our annual show of greed and Mom and Dad were dazzled by Melanie's lack of it." Lori glanced up and Andy mugged a look that said Melanie's self-denial hadn't lasted. "So they filled the room with yellow balloons. We've had them at Christmas ever since. Every adult within shouting range is usually forced to help blow them up. You escaped too quickly."

"Good instincts," Lori said lightly. "I worked hard on perfecting the art of disappearing at crucial times."

Rather than the smile Lori expected, Andy watched her with troubled eyes.

"It's a lovely tradition." Lori changed the subject back to the balloons and concentrated on the bow she was attaching to a package. Her own Christmas traditions consisted of wondering if anyone would remember to get her something to unwrap and practicing her smile to show it didn't matter if they didn't or if the present wasn't exactly suitable. The Barbie doll she'd received when she was fourteen had taught her to disappear when smiling grew too difficult.

She glanced back at the stocking with her name on it and swallowed hard. The festive room, the tree, the way Andy was looking at her, the stocking with her name—

spelled correctly—all made Lori want to cry. Kris's memories of Christmas wouldn't be like hers, she thought fiercely.

"In a few years, Kris will be bringing home ornaments she's made in school," Andy promised softly, reading her mind. "Your tree will shrink before your eyes till they all won't fit. And you'll add more and more traditions of your own every year."

"I hope so," she whispered half to herself, absently picking up another package.

"Why did you grow up in foster homes, Lori? What happened to your parents?"

"Is this something that will help our case?" She looked up at him hopefully.

He grinned. "Curiosity. Pure and simple."

"Oh." Lori studied the sticky stuff on the back of another bow with more attention than it required. She'd known someone in Andy's family would ask eventually. People always did. And they usually prefaced it with "If you don't mind me asking", which meant they knew they should mind their own business.

She grinned inside at some of the stories she'd concocted over the years in order to escape pity. She wondered if Andy would appreciate the "mother dead/father in the diplomatic corps" one. He'd earned the truth.

The room suddenly felt cold. "I don't really know much about my father. He left Mom before he knew about me and was a semiforbidden subject." Lori shivered. "My mother said she had loved him too much. Talking about him was too painful. I learned quickly not to ask any question that caused her too much pain."

"I don't understand—"

"She was an alcoholic," Lori said. "She couldn't hold a job, couldn't take care of me while I was growing up." She focused on taping ribbon to a present. "I'd live with her for a while, something would start her up, she would go on one of her binges and then someone would pick me up and take me somewhere else.''

"Place you in foster care, you mean?''

Lori barely paused to nod. "She'd get help, get sober,'' she continued, "then they'd declare her well and I'd live with her until she fell off the wagon again and did something they thought might endanger me. They'd take me again and I'd live with another family, go to another school.'' She took a deep breath. "She loved me. I have no doubt she loved me. That doesn't mean her actions didn't have adverse effects on my life.''

"What happened to her?'' Andy asked.

"She drank herself to death when I was sixteen.''

There was a long silence. "Growing up that way must have been difficult.'' His soothing voice seemed to come from a far, far distance.

"After she died, I lived in one home two whole years, until I was eighteen and no longer a ward of the court.'' She smiled reminiscently. "Sharon and I turned eighteen a week apart and got our first apartment together. We worked two jobs each, got college loans, took a few classes. The years after my mother died were the most stable of my life.''

"Kris's life will be stable,'' Andy assured her. Kris had finished her bottle and Andy had turned her against his shoulder. Kris was curled into a tiny little ball, braced by his strong arm. She looked right there, her eyes closed, so peaceful.

"You sound more optimistic than Melanie and John did,'' Lori said, putting her leftover odds and ends of ribbon back in the sack.

"They have to ask all the questions, cover every possible thing that could trip you up,'' Andy said.

"You don't think I'm going to lose her?''

"My father and Mel don't, either."

Lori tried not to look skeptical. Her heart thundered in her chest as she tried not to hope too hard.

"We talked more before we went to bed," Andy went on.

Lori could imagine the three of them, heads together, whispering at the top of the stairs about precedents and legal technicalities while everyone else got exasperated and went to bed without them.

"Speaking of bed," Veronica said from the door, "you two should be heading there. It looks like Kris is asleep and morning is going to come awfully early."

"Mom has this thing for the old 'early to bed, early to rise' adage," Andy explained with a wry smile that didn't look all that pleased. Lori had a feeling Veronica had arrived just in time. The way he was looking at her made her fidgety.

"I just thought I should make sure everything was okay," Veronica said.

"Everything's fine," Lori said, hurrying toward Andy to get Kris. "And you're right. I know I need to get to bed."

"I'll get the lights in here," Veronica offered.

Andy passed the baby to Lori and followed the two of them down the semidark hall to the den. As Lori would have gone inside, he touched her arm, letting his hand linger. "Don't count on Mom and Kris to rescue you forever, sweet Lori," he warned. Or promised. She wasn't sure. His smile was almost lost in the tiny bit of light escaping from the family room. "Sweet dreams."

Christmas morning came much too slowly.

Andy's mother had sabotaged his plans last night, sending them both back to bed like little kids. This morning, he'd had twenty minutes with Lori—and that had been used in caring for Kris—before the rambunctious crew was up, demanding that everyone else get up, too. Santa had obviously arrived and it was time to open presents.

However impatient Andy felt, he watched with satisfaction as Lori opened her presents. Her quiet delight was every bit as real as his niece's and nephews' noisy glee. The sweater from his mother extracted an amazed appreciation from her. The used how-to-care-for-baby book brought tears to her eyes as Lori hugged it to her and thanked Melanie in a husky voice.

The silky robe he'd bought her earned him a silent thank-you that made him burn inside.

He'd bought the robe with a fantasy of taking it off her firmly fixed in the back of his mind. The old ratty one she wore testified that she probably didn't make a habit of entertaining "guests". Now his palms grew sweaty when he thought she might not make an exception for him. The plan that had seemed so perfect yesterday seemed faulty, at best, today.

Lori dashed away big tears as she opened Kris's presents. She sniffed and stabbed at a couple more when his father turned his back to her after distributing the Christmas stockings. Andy gnashed his teeth and wished this public Christmas would be over. He couldn't wait for the private one he planned later and was certain the tiny box in his pocket would soon burn a hole in his jeans.

He resented his mother's drawn-out Christmas rituals. They lingered over breakfast too long. They played with the kids and put puzzles together endlessly.

As the day wore on, he watched Lori skirt sideways through doorways with mistletoe hung over them without the least hesitation. She avoided being alone with him for even a second. With the house so full, it wasn't difficult. She gradually withdrew as tomorrow came closer.

By the time they finally sat down to their traditional late-afternoon Christmas dinner, he was so close to bursting with impatience, he couldn't eat.

Seeing Lori push the food around her plate, not enjoying the meal any more than him, didn't bring a bit of comfort.

"Thank you so much for having me and Kris, Veronica," Lori finally said. "This is the nicest Christmas I've ever had."

"There'll be others," his mother promised, squeezing Lori's hand. Andy tried not to feel jealous of their easy affection. Wasn't that everything he'd hoped for when he'd brought her here?

Andy rose slowly and Lori took the hint. "We need to go," he told the room in general. He looked at Melanie as he added, "Busy day tomorrow."

Melanie nodded in agreement and promised to be at the courthouse by eight the next morning and be in touch by nine. She'd let them know what she had accomplished.

The goodbyes were lengthy. It was almost seven by the time Lori zipped her coat and wrapped Kris in her blanket. Kris, exhausted from the day's activities and being passed around, barely stirred as they strapped her seat in the back of the car.

Andy had the engine running while he'd packed the car. It was warm, too warm, he thought, unzipping his coat a little as he backed down the long driveway.

"You have a wonderful family," Lori murmured. "I'll never forget this Christmas."

Automatically, he reached over and smoothed her soft hair. "Yeah. I heard you tell my mother." Knowing they were alone again—except for Kris—filled him with anticipation.

He braked at a stoplight and glanced back at the baby. She still slept soundly. His gaze returned to Lori and found her watching him. Slightly flustered at being caught, she flushed and focused quickly on the red traffic light.

He felt the corners of his mouth turn up in a cocky smile but couldn't help it. Blaming the box in his pocket for making his jeans uncomfortably tight, he rolled down his window an inch to catch a whiff of the crisp, cold air.

The light changed and he pressed the accelerator with more force than he intended. He could hardly wait to get on with his plans.

Lori gave Andy an uncertain smile as they stopped in front of their apartment building a short time later.

"You get Kris," he suggested. "I'll unload the car."

By the time he'd delivered the tower of presents and baby things to her apartment, Lori had settled into the corner of the couch to hold a sleeping Kris.

"What next?" he asked as he set the last box near the arch between the foyer and the living room.

"Go home," she said simply.

His stance widened, making him look braced for battle. He looked immovable. His gaze paused on her lips and they tingled in memory of his kiss the other night.

"You think you're going to get rid of me that easily?"

She felt her smile tilt. "I didn't say it would be easy."

He sobered. "You want to be alone tonight?"

She wished. Oh, how she *wished* that were the case. She wanted to *beg* him to stay. Her insides quaked with the thought of being here alone. She wanted him to hold her like she was holding Kris.

"No," she said truthfully. "Oh, Andy, every time I think past tomorrow, I get so frightened." Her hand shook as she smoothed Kris's blanket.

She glanced up to see Andy's eyes darken. He shifted abruptly. For a moment, the confident and self-assured man seemed uncertain. He looked from her to Kris, then gently took the baby. "Wait," he instructed, lifting one finger. "She's asleep. I'm putting her in your bed." He returned without the baby a minute later and extended his hands. She took them, frowning as he tugged her up from the couch. His eyes held an unreadable glint as he took her into his arms. "At least let me hold you, take some of the fear away."

She sighed and let him grant her wish. She felt safe, protected—and aware, so aware of him.

He stroked her head and she let him push it against his shoulder. His butter-soft sweater was warm, tantalizing against her cheek. She could still smell the faint scent of the aftershave he'd worn all day.

"What are we going to do if we can't get the emergency hearing before Judge Benson?" Lori regretted the quiver in her voice. Her eyes closed in exquisite peace when his arms tightened.

"We'll request him, but once we request the emergency hearing, we have to take whomever we get."

"Is that bad? Do you know how early the hearing will be scheduled?" she remembered to ask, thankful for anything that kept her from thinking about the solid, sweet sound of his heartbeat beneath her ear.

"Probably not until afternoon. One or two o'clock if we're lucky. Especially after a holiday. Does it matter?"

"I need time to call the hotel I told you about. I'm going to accept the job they offered me if it's still open. Won't that increase my chances? Make me look better?"

He leaned away from her. "Is that what you want to

do, Lori? Even if your boss calls and changes his mind about firing you?''

"I've been thinking about it ever since Melanie suggested my traveling could be a problem," she said. "I also spend a lot of weekends and evenings working. That was one of the reasons I loved that job. It filled the time when I wasn't doing anything else. If I have Kris, I don't need to fill time, do I?''

"Babies don't usually leave you a lot of extra time to spare," he agreed. "And a guaranteed job, with very little travel?" He waited for her nod. "That will definitely help eliminate some of the negatives."

He wrapped her in his arms again and they stood silently for a long moment.

"What convinced you that you can't have children, Lori?''

She felt his breath, his words, filter through her hair. She'd known she couldn't avoid the subject forever. He'd been itching with it all day. And last night.

"When I was fifteen, shortly before my mother died," she started, "I had a severe infec—''

"I don't mean physically," he interrupted impatiently. "I mean, why did you discard the idea of adopting?" He swayed her in his arms just as if he was rocking Kris. That and the tone of his voice soothed her. "You obviously didn't consider that an option but now you're willing to adopt Kris."

"That's different."

"How? Did you think you couldn't love someone else's child as much as you could a child of your own?''

"I can't imagine how I could love Kris more if she were my own. It seems fated, as if she's supposed to be with me."

"Does the fact that you can't have kids have anything to do with your...your...decision—" he leaned back, scowling at her as if that wasn't the word he wanted but he couldn't think of a better one ''—not to marry? Is that why you don't form close relationships?''

Lori shook her head in disbelief and gazed up at him. He'd actually listened to every word she'd ever spoken.

''You don't allow yourself to? Is infertility the barrier you put up for anyone who gets too close? Is that how you avoid close relationships?''

A rush of resentment filled the space in her heart that had been overflowing with warmth for him a minute ago. ''It's called honesty, Andy.'' She withdrew from his arms and saw—pity?—in his eyes. ''I thought we'd agreed not to talk about this?''

''I didn't agree.'' He pulled her back into his embrace.

''Andy...'' She raised her head.

He grazed her mouth with a light kiss, silencing her. Her blood raced dizzyingly through her veins. She felt his heart in the hand pressed between them against his chest. Or maybe it was her pulse hammering in her fingertips. She couldn't tell anymore.

One of his hands curved around to her neck and cradled her head, which suddenly felt light. She savored the pleasant tremor that ran down her back as he sank his fingers into her short hair. His brown eyes heated with desire and clashed determinedly with hers. ''As your lawyer, I couldn't do this.''

His lips slowly touched here, there, burning a path down her throat, across her cheek, to her eyes. Her fingers tightened on his shoulders.

He laced his fingers through the belt at her waist as if he was afraid of where his hands might go if they weren't tethered. ''Or this.'' Brushing her mouth with his again, he lingered, parting her lips with his tongue as he deepened the kiss.

She wanted nothing more than to get lost in the sensations that threatened her resolve. She grasped for her much-prized common sense.

"I'm not your lawyer now and you push me away with an excuse?" He said the word as if it were a curse, giving her just enough time to gasp for air before he kissed her again.

Her knees went weak. She fought her reaction to him. She had to think. An excuse. Andy needed children. Seeing him with his niece and nephews had hammered it home. He couldn't have them with her. "Andy…"

His lips settled on an especially sensitive spot behind her ear. She groaned and couldn't remember what she'd wanted to say.

Andy reminded her. "What? You want to remind me you can't have kids?" he asked gruffly. He planted a kiss on the skin just inside the collar of her shirt. "Is that supposed to make me run in the other direction? Make me stop wanting to do this?" He returned his attention to her mouth. "Is that the plan?"

"Yes," she managed. It took every bit of her strength to finally push herself away.

Everything about him said he wanted to settle down. His house. His longing to move ahead in his career, to be appointed a judge. His obvious desire for stability. His reverence for family. Kids and marriage had to be a part of that picture.

There was no doubt in her mind that he'd been seeing her in a possible starring role. Kris, too. She'd felt it when he'd taken her to his house. If she hadn't told him the truth, he would have been parading her before his parents all day. She wondered if an inspection tour was the original intent behind his invitation to join his family.

Life was so unfair. She wanted to apologize. She wasn't certain for what.

He dropped one hand to his side. The other he used to comb a hand through his thoroughly mussed hair. "I liked what was happening between us," he protested.

Her throat burned with unshed tears for his use of the past tense. In her whole life, she'd never wanted something so badly, especially something she knew she couldn't have.

"You want a nice stable life, Andy. A family. Is it wrong for me to want you to have that?"

"You're right. That's what I want." His eyes held hers. "I also want you."

She couldn't look at him. She heard the hunger in his voice and knew it would be reflected in her eyes.

"Once I knew the facts," he continued, "I was supposed to stop wanting to explore the possibilities with you?"

Unlike him, she had no desire to explore impossible possibilities. "There aren't any," she said. "That's the whole point."

He laughed without humor. "Oh," he mocked. "Seems the little bombshell you dropped yesterday morning increases the possibilities." A slight bitterness crept into his voice. "We can explore all sorts of possibilities with only a fraction of the worries we'd have if…things…were normal." He let his gaze wander inch by inch down her body. "A built-in opportunity to play without pay, without risking a thing."

She felt stripped, unclothed.

There was an anger in his eyes she didn't understand. He caught her hands. "I want you. Don't tell me you're not interested," he continued. "I won't believe it."

She couldn't say a word.

"Marry me."

The words caught her off guard. They were totally unexpected.

"Marry me, Lori. Then we can both have what we want."

"You can't keep saying that," she protested.

"Don't I get the courtesy of an answer?"

"You're serious," Lori challenged him quietly. "You think we should talk about getting married?"

"I don't think we should talk about it." His voice was staccato. "I think we should do it."

He hadn't said a thing about how he felt. She was glad. This all had to do with desire on his side and Kris on hers. Kris for him, too, she realized numbly. Why should she be surprised that he was caught up in wanting Kris as much as she did? She'd seen the way he was with his niece and nephews. He spread his love for babies and kids around like sunshine. And except for actually finding Kris, Andy had been as involved as she'd been with the beautiful baby. "For Kris?" she felt compelled to clarify, pulling away from him.

He didn't say anything for a long moment. "I want Kris," he admitted, his voice rough with emotion, something she didn't think he intended.

"Oh, Andy, I haven't been thinking about anyone but me. I didn't think about how you might feel."

He looked sad. "I know." He leaned and kissed the tip of her nose.

"Did you discuss this option with Melanie and your dad?" Lori ventured closer to him. "I know you mean well, Andy. I know you think you're eliminating negatives but...I do not expect a human sacrifice," she added. She lifted her hand toward him, then froze. She wanted to touch him as much as she'd ever wanted anything. It was agony.

"Is that what you think?" He caught her fingers and pressed her palm against his chest, over his heart, exactly where she'd wanted to put it. "I am not offering myself as a sacrifice." He lifted her fingers and kissed the tips.

"But what could *you* possibly gain?" she asked more wistfully than she intended, pulling her tingling hand away from him.

"A wife." His jaw hardened into a dangerous line. "A child."

"Permanently?" She was still stunned by the entire conversation.

Her question obviously annoyed him. "You know people who consider marriage temporary?"

Lori's mind had quit working several minutes ago. She didn't know anything right now.

"You...you aren't looking at this as one of our legal options?" She clipped her words.

He seemed insulted. Somehow, she'd gotten his back up again, offended him. "I don't think changing wives every few years would enhance my chances of being appointed to the bench. Do you?"

She suddenly understood. He was looking at the whole package. The desire that was so obviously there between them. Kris. The stable image he'd been busily creating. "You think I'll look good on your résumé. Like your house."

"Dammit, Lori. Dammit, Lori," he repeated more softly.

How could he look so irritated when he'd kissed her a minute ago with such tenderness? But she was glad. If he stayed this way, she wouldn't weaken and listen to his divine foolishness. She wouldn't think about how wanted and wonderful she'd felt in his arms.

"You know what makes me angry?" His eyes snapped and his voice lowered menacingly.

"I have no idea."

"You always sell yourself short, Lori," he went on.

"Too short. Somewhere along the line, you've decided if you don't expect too much, you won't be disappointed. You don't have to take any chances." He crowded her, forcing her to take a step backward.

"You can't lose something you never had, Andy. That's what I keep telling you. It can't hurt to lose something if you don't have it in the first place." She licked her dry lips. "I'm thinking of your dreams, too."

"How noble. So you're protecting *me*?"

She frowned, shaking her head. "No, Andy. I'm protecting myself. You're right. I'm not willing to risk... getting involved with you."

"So you're only concerned with yourself?"

"That isn't... Yes. Oh, I don't know."

"Is your concern for Kris selfish, too?"

The room turned icy with the question.

"Do you only want her because she's your only shot at motherhood?"

Wrapping her arms around herself, Lori slipped past him. She sank onto the couch because her knees wouldn't hold her any longer. "My...*this*," she amended, "has nothing to do with my wanting Kris. I hadn't thought about the fact that I couldn't have kids until—" Stunned, she broke off abruptly.

She'd been about to say until she fell in love with him. The truth slammed into her. She couldn't deny it. Against her best judgment, despite her best efforts, she'd fallen in love with him. He was everything she would have wanted if she'd allowed herself to think of marriage.

And it was hopeless.

"Until?" He drew it out, waiting.

She schooled her features. She'd had lots of practice at not giving herself away. "Until you kissed me. I realized there was...there did seem to be...some...thing happening between us.''

''Chemistry?'' He mocked her.

She understood his disgust. He felt duped. Conned. Something he wanted had been dangled before him but he'd found out it wasn't real. It was plastic. And he wanted her anyway. The same way she wanted him.

She was too proud to deny her reaction to him when he could plainly see and feel it. ''I thought it only fair that you knew the facts before things progressed any further.''

''Forewarned is forearmed?''

She nodded. ''Maybe we should have an affair. Get it out of our system.'' The very thought made her weak. She wanted to crumble at his feet. ''Let's have...sex and...and...''

''I want to make love with you,'' he assured her in a quiet voice that sounded ominous, threatening. ''But wouldn't that ruin your whole take on my proposal?''

He'd changed the words. Somehow, calling it ''making love'' instead of ''sex'' turned the discussion deadly serious.

He crossed his arms over his chest. His tone was wry. ''Having an affair wouldn't help our chances of keeping Kris.''

''Andy, I think...'' She *couldn't* think. A mishmash of emotions assaulted her and clouded her usually sensible thoughts. No matter how much she wanted and wished and would love to marry him, she had to face facts. ''I'd be cheating you.''

He compressed his lips. ''Why don't you let me be the judge of that?''

''We should wait *until* we know if I get to keep Kris,'' she suggested blithely. ''If we do, maybe I wouldn't feel like I was...''

His nostrils flared slightly. She saw his hands clench. Whatever she'd said, it had transformed his irritation to anger. Thunderclouds formed behind his eyes.

He looked disgusted. He stepped toward her. "Cheating?" he finished for her.

She couldn't listen anymore. She wanted to put her hands over her ears and shut him out. She stood and pushed past him. "Your problem is, you expect *too* much. I'll bet you've never had anything that didn't fall into your lap. Now you just expect it. Welcome to real life, buddy. Better a little pain now than a lot later."

She stumbled out of the room. He didn't try to stop her.

CHAPTER TEN

LORI leaned against the door she closed behind her, trembling like a leaf. She had to get through the night. How dare Andy distract her.

A sob escaped her throat. She choked it back. She would not cry. She just wouldn't. Andy lived in some fantasyland, one she couldn't afford to even consider visiting.

Tiptoeing to the other side of the room, she watched Kris sleep and tried not to feel desolate. She touched Kris's cheek and wondered if babies who went without love smiled in the same sweet way when they were touched. At least Kris had love. For now.

She shook her head. She couldn't think about what she would do if she had to give up Kris, too. *Oh, Andy.* Her heart felt as if it would break.

She heard him moving around the living room, prowling. He came once to stand outside the bedroom door. She waited, holding her breath, for him to knock, not sure what she would do when he did. If he persisted with his crazy scheme, she wasn't certain she'd be able to resist him. Surely she deserved what he was offering, even if he didn't deserve the little she could give him in return.

Let me be the judge, he'd said.

She wished she could.

He came once more to her door and knocked lightly. "I'm leaving, Lori." He paused, waiting for what seemed like forever. "I'll call you in the morning as soon as I hear from Melanie."

She stood still, transfixed, until she heard the apartment door open and close.

When she was sure he'd gone, she didn't hold back the wishes and regrets. Just the tears.

Let me be the judge, he'd said.

Oh, how she wished she could.

Andy called by a quarter after eight the next morning. Melanie had managed to get Judge Benson, he reported in a flat, even voice. Their hearing was scheduled for eleven.

The grayish white stone courthouse matched the cold gray day. Despite the county's attempt at spreading Christmas cheer, the huge wreath on the clock tower looked dead and bleak.

Lori shivered as Andy led her up the steps, his hand pressed lightly beneath her arm. He'd acted like a stranger ever since he'd picked them up. It didn't change as he held the door for them. "Nervous?"

Lori could only nod. Her mouth felt dry enough to imitate a desert. If he'd only smile, it would help.

"Andy?" she started as they stood before the elevator, waiting.

He met her eyes for the first time since his arrival at her apartment.

"Andy," she started again, "I am sorry about last night." She licked her lips. "I...know you were trying to be...helpful."

Andy winced and looked straight ahead as the elevator doors swept silently open.

She felt his hand on the small of her back, even through her heavy coat, as he waited to follow her inside.

"I do want you to know I appreciate...everything. Everything you've done," she whispered as the doors closed them in.

Andy's eyes bored into her. Then he looked at Kris. "You were right last night," he said after a moment. His jaw hardened into granite. "I would feel cheated."

Something inside her plummeted. How she could be disappointed when he'd just agreed she'd won their argument, she wasn't sure.

Andy steered her out of the elevator toward the courtroom, where Melanie said she would meet them. A woman turned as they neared and Lori recognized his mother. Veronica McAllister's warm smile made up a little bit for the chilly distance Andy had put between them despite their proximity.

Veronica hurried toward them. "You're here." Tugging back Kris's blanket, she smiled at the sleeping baby. "Everyone's waiting." She pressed a quick kiss on Kris's forehead almost automatically.

"Thank you for coming," Lori managed to say.

"Everyone?" Andy asked.

"Everyone," Veronica answered. "Well, except Jeff. He stayed home with the kids. John thought it might look good for all of us to be here." She herded them toward the courtroom. "Judge Benson might be influenced to make a more favorable decision if he sees you have so much support." She directed her last remark to Lori, adding dryly, "As if John could have kept us away."

The courtroom was small, circular. Platformlike steps lined with visitors' benches led down into something resembling a pit.

Melanie sat in the "arena" at a large oak table to the right of the towering judge's bench, gesturing for them to come down. Allison, John and Greg had spread out, one each on the three benches behind her. The left side of the courtroom was empty.

Veronica patted Lori's arm and slipped into a seat beside John as they passed. When Lori reached the rail separating Melanie's table from the rest of the room, she suddenly felt alone. Glancing over her shoulder, she saw Andy taking a place in the first row beside Allison.

Lori started to protest, but the look in his eyes stopped her. There was a disquieting hurt there, camouflaged until now by the shadows under his eyes. He looked away and she realized she'd denied him the right to join her.

He stared straight ahead.

Lori's knees shook as she pushed open the small gate. Her arm tightened around Kris.

Melanie guided her into the seat beside her as a door behind the raised judge's bench opened. As a small entourage came in and took their places, Lori watched the judge. Her first impression was gray—thick gray hair with a mind of its own, bushy gray brows, gray complexion, as if he rarely saw the sun. The stark black robe did nothing to change the impression. His kindly, animated blue eyes did.

His gaze swept the courtroom behind her, stopping for a nod at John, then Andy. He finally turned his attention on her and Melanie.

Then everything happened pretty much as Melanie had said it would. It all seemed surreal until the judge aimed his startling blue eyes on Lori and asked the questions Melanie, Andy and John had warned her to expect.

"Ms. Warren, do you have any reason to believe this child's mother chose *you*? Was the baby left with you for a specific reason?"

"I thought so at first," Lori admitted.

"A relative perhaps? A friend who might trust you exclusively?"

"I can't think of anyone it might be."

"And no specific reason?"

She shook her head. There were legions of reasons why anyone who knew her well would *not* choose her.

"Why then, Ms. Warren, didn't you report finding the baby to the proper authorities?"

The questions went on, each one harder than the last to answer. An ominous feeling made Lori's heart too heavy for her chest long before Judge Benson's gavel thundered once against his desk.

"The petitioner's request for guardianship is denied."

Reality cracked Lori's heart at the words.

Melanie went forward to get papers the court clerk extended to her. Lori sat silently in her place, trying to accept that the judge had taken back the precious gift someone had given her.

With a last compassionate grimace in Lori's direction, Judge Benson flowed quickly out of the room.

"Oh, Lori," Veronica and Allison cried in unison. Andy's hand closed over her shoulder. "I'm sorry," she heard Melanie say.

With tears streaming down her face, Lori's hold on Kris tightened as Andy wrapped his own empty arms around both of them. He waited patiently for her emotional storm to pass, handing her a tissue when it did. She felt his helplessness in the words he didn't say.

"There are additional things we can do," Andy assured her when she finally pulled away. "Steps we can take."

"Yeah." Melanie's hopeful voice came from what seemed far, far away. Lori looked over Andy's shoulder to see Melanie settling back at the table. She and John flipped pages in the document she'd been given. Her expression brightened. "Judge Benson will review Lori's request in six weeks to see if she has met the county's requirements to become a foster parent," she told the room in general.

Andy drove them silently back to the apartment complex. Someone from social services would pick up Kris and her things sometime this afternoon, they'd been informed.

"What can I do?" Andy asked as he unlocked Lori's apartment door for them.

"Just be here," Lori said without hesitation.

"That I can do."

Lori went to lay Kris on her bed.

Andy was waiting when she returned to the hall. Her hand shook as she pushed her bangs back off her forehead. It took every bit of strength she had left to look him in the eyes. "I'd better pack Kris's things."

"Lori—"

"You were right. I messed up when I didn't call the authorities." She held up a hand. "I thank you from the bottom of my heart for everything. Everything." She had to stop and clear her throat. "I know this hasn't been easy for you, either. I...I know you love Kris, too." She tried to offer him a smile, knowing it was weak at best.

"Just tell me what I can do to help." He pushed himself away from the wall.

She was grateful to him for not holding her weaknesses and self-pity against her. "If you'd like, you can get the box," she said. "I think most of her stuff is still in it from the trip to your mother's. I'll check around for the rest of her things."

He nodded.

"What next?" he asked ten minutes later when, with all the Christmas presents, they had three boxes jammed full.

Lori drew a shaky breath and released it on a long sigh. "I don't know." She shrugged helplessly. "If you don't want to hang around, if you want to leave…"

He shook his head mutely. "Not unless you want me to."

Her gut reaction was yes. She didn't want him watching her heart break. Her goodbyes to both of them might be easier in private. But the last thing she wanted was to be alone. And she could say her silent goodbyes to him at the same time she said them to Kris. "No." She shook her head.

His heartfelt thanks surprised her.

"I think maybe I'll just hold Kris until…"

He nodded. "Good idea."

He held both of them as they sat on the couch together. For endless moments, she let herself lose her quiet grief for Kris in him. Then it turned into grief *for* him.

Lori was torn between wanting the ordeal to be over so this pain would evolve to numbness and wanting time to stand still.

They talked quietly about everything except Kris. Or her and him.

Both of them straightened as the doorbell pealed all too soon. A minute ago, Lori wouldn't have believed her heart could beat any faster or harder. It showed her it could.

"I'll get it," Andy said, touching a finger to Kris's tiny mouth as he rose.

"This is it," Lori whispered and hugged Kris to her

breast. She closed her eyes and memorized the feel of the tiny body curled so trustingly against hers.

You're going to have a wonderful life, she thought with all her might, trying to imprint it on Kris's brain. *You will. You will.*

"Lori?" Andy's voice was soft.

She opened her eyes.

Reluctantly, Lori handed the baby across to the matronly-looking woman who was irritatingly official beneath all her smiles. Andy was there, helping. His hand gripped hers and his eyes carried an encouraging smile.

Lori was very careful not to touch the babe when she handed the social worker the bottle she'd prepared for the feeding that would soon be due.

"What are you going to do now?" he asked when Kris was gone. She stumbled into him and his arms circled her waist.

Lori couldn't even form a complete thought. "I don't know," she whispered. "I don't know. I guess I'll go on like I was before she came."

He pulled her closer, shaping her to his body. His breath against her neck felt warm and comforting. His quiet strength seeped through her, settling into her bones. She wanted to lose herself in his strong arms, bury her face in his hard, broad chest and draw more of it. His lips moved against her neck and he tightened his hold as if to cushion her until some of the trembling stopped.

He held on to her a long, long time. His arms warmed her in places she felt chilled and empty. She buried her face in his shoulder.

Then his lips brushed her forehead lightly and she finally managed to push herself away. If she wasn't careful, the emotions of the past few hours would blind her and scramble her thinking. No, his touch alone was enough to do that, she realized. She hadn't thought clearly since last night.

She lifted her chin. "This is the hardest thing I've ever done," she said, pleased with herself that she succeeded in tacking a half smile on the end. "Comfort is probably beyond the call of duty," she added brightly. "I hope you'll tell someone from your office to add it to the bill."

The look Andy gave her bordered on disgust. "I'm sure Melanie will be in touch." The stranger who had picked her up this morning had returned. With a vengeance.

"Good," Lori said, nodding, and folded her hands.

"Then…" His lips compressed in a thin, straight line. "I guess you don't need me any longer."

Lori's heart protested. How could she pretend anymore? She wanted the other Andy back. The caring one. The friend. "Could we…?" She started over. "Andy, I don't want…I mean…I want—"

He held up his hands, stopping her. More than a tinge of anger crept into his voice. "Whatever you're thinking, I would make a *lousy* consolation prize."

The apartment suddenly felt cold, as if a gust of winter wind had blown through. She shivered.

"I guess I'll see you around."

She nodded again.

With a small salute, he let himself out of her life.

Do you have any reason to believe this child's mother chose you? The question haunted Lori for the next three weeks as she threw herself into her "new" life. She started her new job. She began foster parenting classes. She continued to hope that when she was done, she'd have Kris with her again.

The social worker in charge of Kris's case called at least twice a week to give progress reports and Lori talked to Veronica often. Melanie called twice. Thankfully, neither of them mentioned *him*. She worked hard at not thinking about Andy.

It was impossible.

Only pride had kept her away from the physical fitness facility in the basement of the apartment complex clubhouse, and she'd gone instead to the gym by the mall. Until Kris, the complex workout room was the only place she'd run into him.

One day she saw him constructing a snowman outside his apartment with Michael, Melanie's son. She watched from behind the vertical blinds covering her sliding glass door, moving only once—when Andy glanced up—in the hour or two they were out.

She'd done him such an injustice, she realized. How could she have thought he'd have to have children of his own to be happy? Could he laugh any more merrily than he did when he swung Michael around and gently tossed him in a snowdrift? Could he show anymore joy as he bent to let the four-year-old boy's snowball hit him? Could he love his own kids any more than he so evidently loved his niece and nephews? Or Kris?

Lori only had to close her eyes to visualize Kris sleeping in his arms, barely making her mark against the expanse of his broad shoulder. She could see Kris's soft smile as she dreamed the sweet dreams Andy had wished on her, dreams of being loved and secure. Tears filled Lori's eyes and clogged her throat.

The second Saturday in January, she saw a moving van parked outside the building.

Mid-January. That was about when he'd said his house would be finished, she recalled with a panicky dismay. She knew she couldn't let it end like this. Not with that cold goodbye the day after Christmas. The day they'd taken Kris.

She missed him as much as she missed Kris—even more, she admitted honestly for once.

Not giving herself time to think about it, she hurried into the bathroom and tried to do something with her Saturday hair. She smoothed on a little makeup. In the mirror, she rehearsed and discarded inane things to say when she got to his apartment.

She'd wasted her time. The men packing Andy's things said he wasn't there. He'd left everything ready for them and was meeting them at his house this afternoon, they informed her.

With a heart as heavy as anything she'd ever known, Lori headed for the elevator at the end of the hall. She rarely used it but she didn't have the energy to face the stairs again.

"Wait, Miss Warren."

Lori turned to see the building's busybody hurrying toward her, waving a small piece of paper in her hand. Bertha Thomas was a widow who lived in the apartment directly across from Andy's.

"I have his address," she said as she approached. "He's going to have some type of get-together for all of us in that grand new house of his this spring. Asked me to help plan it," she finished proudly.

Lori felt her breath grow shallow. She could find his house, she realized. She'd been there. Nothing could stop her going there anytime she pleased. But it would certainly be easier with his new address in hand.

And it would be easier now that she understood what had been bugging her about the question the judge had asked. Kris's mother hadn't chosen her! Knowing that was important.

Lori groped around her as the elevator doors came open, then slid closed again. "May I borrow this?" She lifted the paper and pressed it to her chest. "I'll bring it back. I don't have my purse. I'll write it down and—"

"I wrote it down for you. That's yours," Mrs. Thomas told her, so pleased to be helpful. "I heard you asking the moving men and thought you might need it. I'm sure Mr. McAllister won't mind," she added.

"He won't. I'm certain," Lori said, heading for the stairs. "I could ask his mother," she added, walking backward. "I know her." She was reassuring herself as much as Mrs. Thomas. All sorts of possibilities sprouted in her mind. "Thanks, Mrs. Thomas. I…" She stopped. "Thanks." She raced up the stairs to the third floor to get her purse and coat, not sure why she'd taken so long to come to her senses.

When she was ready to leave again, she stopped at the door of her apartment, suddenly nervous. She should change clothes, put on something nicer. She knew she was stalling. She'd been stalling for three weeks.

If Andy refused to listen, there wasn't anything she could do. She couldn't blame him, she thought as she made her way to her car.

"I guess you don't need me any longer," he'd said the last time she'd seen him and she hadn't told him how much she did. She'd let him walk out of her life.

At least now she understood why.

Andy's heart stopped the moment he turned into the cul-de-sac in his new neighborhood. A black Mustang sat in his driveway, a Mustang he recognized far too well from spending too much time noting when it came and went at the apartment complex.

The old ticker soared, then settled into a heavy, thundering beat that changed to a sky dive into his stomach when the taillights came on and her car slowly started to reverse. Andy leaned on his horn, swung into his driveway behind her and screeched to a stop, only half-caring if she stopped of her own volition or by hitting his car. Her brake lights glinted, but the relief he felt had nothing to do with avoiding a fender bender.

Setting his parking brake, he watched her hungrily and took a deep breath. It took a moment for him to put on his Iron Man disguise so he could greet her. He climbed from his car. His open coat flapped around him but he didn't feel the cold. The hefty breeze ruffled his hair as he started toward her. He concentrated on turning on his most mellow smile.

She looked fantastic, even with dark, sad circles under her eyes.

"Fancy meeting you here," he said casually as she opened her door.

She had nothing to say.

His courtroom manner almost slipped but he managed to catch it. "Guess you heard I was moving and came to say goodbye?"

She lifted a shoulder and stepped out of the car. He moved away. "Thought it was only fair I get to see your house in the daylight, now that it's finished." She matched her light tone to his but her lip trembled slightly, he noted.

"Then I guess I'd better open the garage door so we can go in." He walked back to his car and punched the remote above the visor.

"Do you want me to move so you can put your car in?" she called breathlessly.

"I'll do it later. After you leave," he added as neutrally as he could, coming toward her again.

She followed him through the garage.

As soon as they were inside, he took her coat, careful not to brush her, careful not to let his hands linger. Letting himself touch her would not help his resolve to forget her. She wasn't interested in the kind of life he had to offer and three long weeks of convincing himself not to waste his time could be wiped out in an instant if he didn't use his head.

"Everything all right? You have news of Kris?"

She gave him a quick, genuine grin. "I think I'm going to get her after all, Andy. Eventually."

Oh, God. That hurt, too. He wanted to be in on "getting" Kris. "That's great, Lori." His voice only rasped a little. He swiveled on one foot. "Guess we'd better get started if we're going to have time for more than the fifty-cent tour." He made a show of glancing at his watch, knowing he would drag the visit out as long as possible. "The movers will be here in less than an hour. Mom and Melanie, too. They're going to help me get settled."

"Andy," she said softly, not following him.

He reluctantly turned back to her. Something in her voice made him *very* reluctant.

"Andy, can we redo the conversation we had that night? Christmas night," she clarified.

The arms he'd crossed over his chest tightened. His fingers bit into flesh.

"The one where you say, 'Marry me and I say—'"

"Why? What's the point, Lori?"

"That's the point. That's what I should have said,

Andy. I should have said 'why' instead of whatever I said.''

"You told me I couldn't keep saying that.''

"I changed my mind. I *want* you to say it again so this time I can say 'why?'''

"Does it make any difference?''

She nodded. "A lot.''

"Why?''

"That's my line.'' She smiled a sad, whimsical smile. "Because I love you, Andy. I'm hoping you love me, too.''

He had trouble keeping his feet fastened to the floor.

"And if you still think you might want me to marry you, then I would very much like a chance to answer again—differently this time,'' she added.

He thought he'd graduated to numbness, but she was making him ache and hurt inside all over again. But hope flowed over the edges of the mix of feelings. He felt it growing in his chest. "Is it all right to ask what brought all of this about?''

Her smile widened a little. Her eyes glimmered with a fine mist of tears. "Where am I going to find someone who's willing to offer me so much in spite of all my flaws?''

He couldn't resist any longer. He opened his arms and she rushed into them.

"Do you love me?'' she whispered.

At the same time, he asked, "What flaws, sweet Lori?'' Then he held her so tight neither of them could think of answers.

He gave up trying. Instead, he gave her the softest, sweetest, most gentle kiss he could manage and prayed it told her what he couldn't yet find words to say.

The one she gave him back stopped his heart but not

his thoughts. "I still don't understand," he admitted against her lips.

He loved the feel of her impish grin pressed against his mouth. "Don't pretend you didn't notice the flaws. You pointed several of them out."

"Such as?" He finally managed to raise his head. Looking at her was almost as good as kissing her. At least it reassured him he wasn't imagining this whole inexplicable fantasy.

"You told me I expect too little at least a dozen times."

"You do."

She sobered, suddenly fascinated with the pattern in his cable-knit sweater. He waited, forcing himself to pretend patience. Whatever she had to say, she was struggling with the words.

"Remember what Judge Benson asked me?" she finally said, veering totally off the subject.

Her hands had slipped to his shoulders. He dipped his head and kissed one of them encouragingly. "What?"

"He asked if I thought Kris's mother had chosen me."

"And you did. You always thought that."

She shook her head slightly. "I wanted to believe it. I guess I finally believe it was just chance."

"I don't—" He clamped his jaws together, realizing she had to explain whatever she'd discovered in her own way.

"I *wanted* to believe it because it was almost like she was really mine. You know?"

He shook his head.

"When you have a baby—the normal way," she added unnecessarily, "you accept what you get. You don't get to choose. You love your kids no matter what.

And your kids have to do the same. Despite your flaws. They *have* to love you."

Tears filled her eyes again and he wanted to take them and shed them for her. She held them back.

"I think I hoped that since Kris didn't get to choose—not really—she just came, like a real kid. I thought she'd *have* to love me. No matter how much she knew about me, she couldn't take it back. No matter how lousy a mother I might be."

He started to protest.

"She'd have to…love me…like I did my mom," she managed to mouth. "And I did love her, despite… despite…"

He let her cry quietly against his shoulder, starting to understand a little bit. Though not the part about loving him. He wasn't sure it mattered anymore. The only thing that mattered was that she did love him.

She finally stopped and pulled away from him, but only arm's length. "When you adopt, you have to go through a process—like the one I'm going through now to become a foster parent." She smiled shakily. "I know they are going to find my flaws. I'm starting to discover that maybe they aren't so major. Maybe I can make up for my weaknesses with the one strength I know I have."

"And what is that?" he asked softly, knowing her answer.

"I have enough love stashed in here—" she pressed her heart "—to spread over a bunch of kids. Whatever happens with Kris," she declared as if warning him, gulping in a deep breath, "I plan on taking on as many as I can handle."

"And that's where I come in," he murmured huskily, giving her a broad wink before he hugged her so close he hoped he'd turn her into a piece of him. She *was* like a part of him, he realized. He'd known it almost from the start.

She'd planted the desire to have her, to share her children that very first evening when he'd watched from the doorway of her bedroom as she became totally enthralled with Kris.

He'd been jealous as hell. He'd thought it was of the man who shared her child. He should have known he was jealous of being left out of her tiny, loving circle. And he'd pushed his way in.

Her tears were almost through. She gazed up at him and trapped him with her dancing, joyful green eyes. "It's going to be awfully difficult to take on a house filled with children when I have to work full time."

He grinned and played along. "And where are you going to put them?" He looked around him and almost chuckled out loud. This little house tour hadn't made it past the utility hall. "Not many will fit in that one-bedroom apartment. I happen to know of a two-bedroom one on the bottom floor of your building that's going to be available very soon."

She pushed a fist into his stomach and then flung herself into his arms again. The overly enthusiastic embrace had much more impact. The kiss that followed was like whipped cream on top of the cake.

He sighed as he lifted his head at last. "I hate to break this to you, Ms. Soon-to-be-mother-of-the-world, but you still haven't said what this has to do with me." He held her face between his hands and searched her eyes. Her arms tightened around his waist as she sobered.

"It scared me to death. I couldn't believe it was true. But I realized you are the one person in the world who *chose* to love me," she finished on a whisper.

His chest and throat were so tight he couldn't breathe.

"Despite my flaws," she added breathlessly. Then her eyes widened. Her mouth opened in a small gape of disbelief, inviting his attention all over again.

She was right. He did choose to love her. In his whole life, he'd never made a wiser decision.

"Except—" her eyes narrowed "—you haven't told me so." She backed away, resting her hands on her shapely hips. "You've let me go on and on and you haven't bothered to say one…"

He couldn't resist touching her any longer. His palm cupped and caressed her cheek. He stole a taste from her sweet lips.

She barely skipped a beat. "No wonder I thought it *was* for Kris. And for this house and because you wanted to get married and be a judge some—"

"I love you, sweet Lori," he interrupted. "I even practiced saying, 'If I had to choose between kids and you, I choose you, Lori.' Then you never gave me a chance to say it."

"Oh, Andy…"

He could get lost in her sighs. And the waterworks looked like they might start again. "That breathless, sexy sigh makes me crazy." He kissed her again. "Marry me?"

"When?" There were stars in her eyes as she stroked a strand of hair from his brow.

"Tomorrow?" He teased her lips with his tongue. "I thought you were supposed to say 'Why?'" he murmured.

She giggled. "Why?"

"Now you're just trying to trick me into saying it again." The doorbell chimed. "Saved by the bell," he quipped, pretending relief.

She turned suddenly serious. "Don't give up on me, Andy."

"Never."

"I promise you won't be sorry."

"I know." He believed it with all his heart. He heard her humming "joyful and triumphant" under her breath as he opened the door. It wasn't even Christmas anymore. It just felt like it.

EPILOGUE

Christmas Eve, one year later

ANDY sighed as Lori slipped into bed beside him. "How's the new one?"

"Finally asleep," Lori whispered, snuggling into Andy's arms, admiring his beloved face. The snow outside the window enhanced the soft moonlight and made the night bright.

"Who would have thought Mom would have to give us a whole wing for our brood in one year?"

Lori could make out his smile in the moon's glow. "Not quite. But we definitely wouldn't have fitted them all in the den."

Kris was officially theirs now. And they had three foster children besides. The three-month-old baby boy she and Veronica had just put to sleep had come only last week.

"Maybe we should have stayed home tonight. We could have driven over tomorrow."

"And miss the balloon blowing?" Andy asked wryly.

Lori giggled. She loved it. She loved Christmas. She loved every little tradition she got to latch on to as a member of the McAllister family. And Kris would love it, too. She had just begun to take her first steps. She would be in ecstasy tomorrow morning when she saw the carpet of yellow balloons, even if she didn't understand that it meant Santa had been there.

"We have the biggest house," she pointed out, rising

to prop herself up on her elbow. "Maybe we should invite them all to our house next year."

"Why do I suspect you'll have the whole thing full by this time next year? We won't have *room* for company."

"We can finish off the basement. Add some bedrooms," she suggested.

Andy growled, surprising her with his agility when she thought he was half-asleep. She was suddenly on her back with his brown eyes glinting down at her.

"Why do I suspect you already have the plans drawn up and stashed somewhere?"

She laughed again, softly, lacing her fingers through his thick dark hair. "Is this your best attempt at cross-examination, Your Honor?"

He kissed her in a way she'd never grow tired of. "I don't do cross-examinations anymore," he muttered. "Just fact-finding. Should I warn you? There's a penalty for lying to the court."

"And what's that?" she teased, breathless at his assault on her senses.

"The same as for telling the truth," he promised, torturing her with a string of kisses down her neck, toward her overly sensitive breasts.

"Good." She sighed. "The truth is...aah...you're making it very hard to concentrate, Your Honor."

"That's the main idea."

"The truth is, I *have* been messing around with a few ideas on paper."

"Gee, what a surprise," Andy mumbled. Lori smiled, then gave herself up to savoring the exquisite sensations he was creating.

"I guess I should be pleased you haven't called in an architect," he said fondly.

"Andy?" she whispered as he returned his attention to her lips.

"Yes?" he said vaguely.

"I'm scheduled to meet with one next week. We do need more space."

"Five bedrooms aren't enough?"

"Maybe not."

Her serious tone finally distracted him from what he was doing. "How many of *these* are we going to adopt?" he asked gently, his full attention on her face.

"I don't know. None of these are eligible for adoption," she reminded him, kissing the place where his dimple usually appeared.

"Did social services call with another one they want us to take?"

"Do you know what a special man you are?" she asked.

He smiled. "Flattery will get you everywhere."

"I know." She loved him as she'd never thought she could love anyone. No matter how hectic his schedule, no matter what was going on in his newly assigned courtroom, he took time every evening to spend individually with each child. He was the dream father many of them would never have again. Of the seven foster children they'd had so far, she had no doubt the four who'd come and gone would remember, that for a while anyway, they were loved. As she was. He gave his love so generously. And always had enough left over for her.

"So what is it you want to tell me?" he urged, suddenly as serious as she felt.

"Since Santa's been here," she said, "I guess I don't have to wait to give you my Christmas present."

Andy jiggled his brows. "How quiet can we be? I

definitely don't want to wake up any babies. Or anyone else.''

"I can be as quiet as the nonstirring mouse your father read about this evening," she whispered. "But it isn't that," she added aloud.

"Darn." He shushed her with another quick kiss. "So tell me. Are we taking in a whole family this time?"

"Just one," she said, almost bursting at the seams with her news. "We're going to have one of our own sometime next July."

Andy was so still for a moment, she was afraid he'd quit breathing. "That...I thought...you said...that wasn't an option," he finally stammered.

"Aren't you pleased?" Her heart raced.

"You're sure?"

She nodded slowly. "Next July. Oh, Andy, I'm sorry to keep springing surprises on you. I didn't know."

He was suddenly laughing. He was on his knees, pulling her up with him, into his arms, rocking and laughing and hugging her till she thought she would die with happiness.

"What happened?" he finally asked.

She shrugged. "I guess the doctor who told me I'd never have babies was wrong. Dr. Fredrickson did say there is scar tissue, that the odds were against it, that it may not happen again, but I *am* pregnant, Andy. Maybe it's just magical you," she added with an adoring sigh. "I hope you're happy."

He reverently touched her stomach. "You know what I love about you?" He gazed into her eyes. "You never fail to amaze me," he said before she could answer. "I love your surprises. I love you."

"Santa's going to be hard-pressed to top *this* next

Christmas,'' he speculated much, much later as he held her in his arms.

Lori didn't say a thing. Santa certainly had been making up for his early failures. Maybe twins? she thought, snuggling deeper into her husband's embrace.

Or maybe she'd give the jolly old elf a rest. The delivery he'd brought her last year—she kissed the tip of Andy's nose—was special enough to last a lifetime.

Question: How do you find the sexy cowboy
of your dreams?

Answer: Read on....

Texas Grooms Wanted!
is a brand-new miniseries from

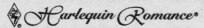

Meet three very special heroines who are all looking for
very special Texas men—their future husbands! Good
men may be hard to find, but these women have experts
on hand. They've all signed up with the Yellow Rose
Matchmakers. The oldest and the best matchmaking service in San Antonio, Texas, the Yellow Rose guarantees
to find any woman her perfect partner....

So for the cutest cowboys in the whole
state of Texas, look out for:

HAND-PICKED HUSBAND
by Heather MacAllister in January 1999

BACHELOR AVAILABLE!
by Ruth Jean Dale in February 1999

THE NINE-DOLLAR DADDY
by Day Leclaire in March 1999

*Only cowboys need
apply...*

Available wherever
Harlequin Romance books
are sold.

In 1999 in Harlequin Romance® marriage is top of the agenda!

Get ready for a great new series by some of our most popular authors, bringing romance to the workplace! This series features gorgeous heroes and lively heroines who discover that mixing business with pleasure can lead to anything...even matrimony!

Books in this series are:

January 1999
Agenda: Attraction! by Jessica Steele

February 1999
Boardroom Proposal by Margaret Way

March 1999
Temporary Engagement by Jessica Hart

April 1999
Beauty and the Boss by Lucy Gordon

May 1999
The Boss and the Baby by Leigh Michaels

Marrying the Boss

From boardroom...to bride and groom!

Available wherever Harlequin books are sold.

HARLEQUIN®
Makes any time special ™

HRMTB

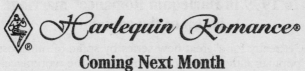

Harlequin Romance®

Coming Next Month

In January look out for a brand-new trilogy featuring the cutest cowboys in the whole state of Texas:

#3535 HAND-PICKED HUSBAND Heather MacAllister
The whole state of Texas seems convinced that Autumn Reese was born to be Clayton Barnett's bride. The whole state bar Clay and Autumn, that is. Which is why she and Clay have dared each other to sign up at the Yellow Rose Matchmakers. Only, watching Clay date other women has made Autumn realize that perhaps her Mr. Right might just be the one she's had within her grasp all along....

Texas Grooms Wanted! is a brand-new trilogy in Harlequin Romance®. Meet three heroines who are all looking for very special Texas men—their future husbands!

Texas Grooms Wanted!: *Only cowboys need apply!*

Also starting in January, find out what happens after office hours in:

#3536 AGENDA: ATTRACTION! Jessica Steele
Edney had been grateful when a handsome stranger had saved her from the unwanted attentions of another man—and amazed when that stranger had kissed her and asked her out to dinner! But Saville Craythorne was not amused. He'd discovered that his new PA was the girl he'd rescued—and he *never* mixed business with pleasure!

Marrying the Boss—*When marriage is top of the agenda!*

#3537 ONLY BY CHANCE Betty Neels
Henrietta's life hadn't been easy. Then, with the help of consultant neurosurgeon Mr. Adam Ross-Pitt, her small world changed irrevocably. He was, of course, far beyond her reach, and if her gratitude to him tipped into love, there was no need for him to know—even if he did keep coming to her rescue!

#3538 MAKE-BELIEVE MOTHER Pamela Bauer and Judy Kaye
Bryan Shepard wanted a mother, and new neighbor Alexis Gordon was perfect for the job. He just had to convince his dad she'd make the perfect wife....

Kids & Kisses—*Where kids and kisses go hand in hand!*